USBORNE

Sandy
Lane
Stables

A Horse for the Summer

Michelle Bates

USBORNE

First published in 1996 by Usborne Publishing Ltd, Usborne House,
83-85 Saffron Hill, London EC1N 8RT, England.
www.usborne.com

First published in America 1996. AE

ISBN 978-0-7945-0501-1 (paperback)

Typeset in Times

Printed in Great Britain

Editor: Susannah Leigh
Series Editor: Gaby Waters
Designer: Lucy Smith
Cover Design: Neil Francis
Map Illustrations: John Woodcock
Cover Photograph supplied by: Only Horses

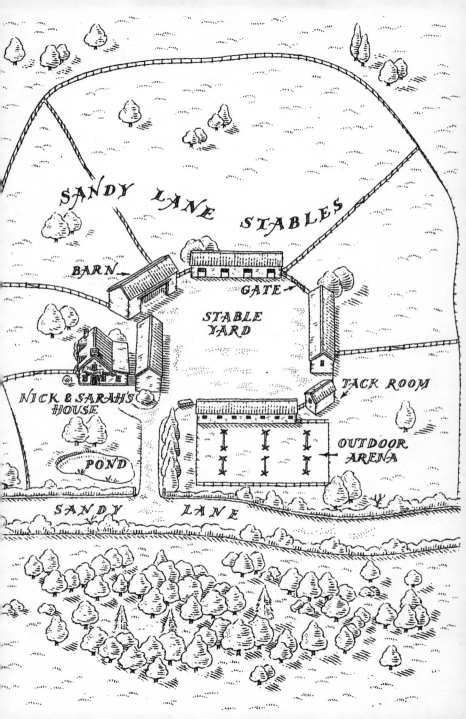

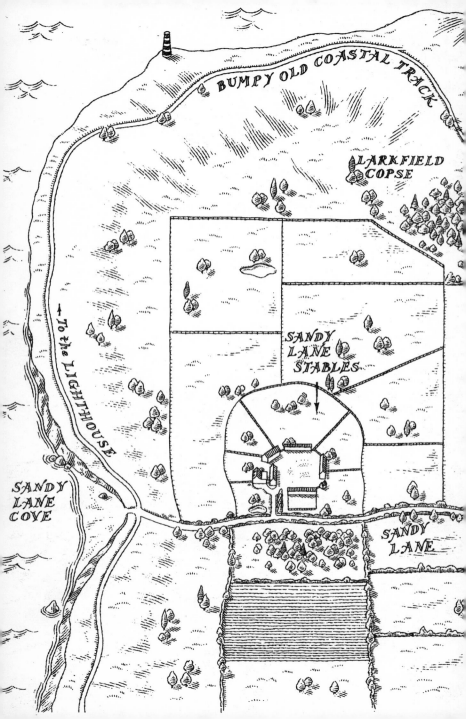

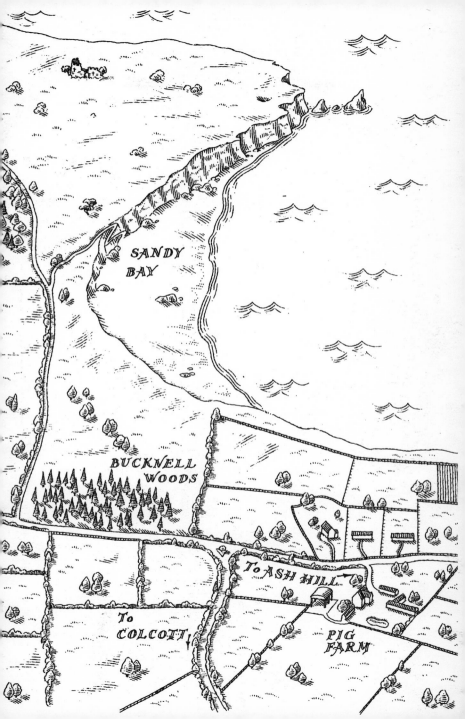

SANDY
BAY

BUCKNELL
WOODS

To ASH HILL

To
COLCOTT

PIG
FARM

CONTENTS

1

EXCITING NEWS

Tom Buchanan pedaled furiously down the drive to Sandy Lane Stables and rattled into the yard. He couldn't believe it had been two years since he'd started riding there. Two whole years... it seemed like only yesterday that he'd first arrived. Time had flown. Yet today was very different from any other day, wonderfully different, for Tom had some very exciting news to share. The early morning mist was rising from the fields as a hazy glow filled the air. Tom jumped off his bike and, throwing it to the ground, charged into the tack room.

"Nick, Sarah, where are you?" he cried, hardly able to contain his excitement. "You're never going to believe my luck." Silence.

Tom called again, only louder this time, but there was still no answer. That was unusual. Nick Brooks and his wife Sarah, the owners of Sandy Lane, could normally be found in the tack room at eight on the dot, carefully planning the day ahead after the early morning feedings.

Tom stood in the doorway and scratched his head. Where was everyone? Twisting slowly around, he scanned the stables. Ah, there was Nick now, coming out of Feather's stall followed by the vet, a burly man with a florid, weather-beaten complexion. Feather had been having trouble with her leg for ages. Tom hoped it wasn't anything serious.

"A sprain in the suspensory ligament... plenty of rest... that's the only thing I can prescribe for her."

Tom could just catch snippets of what the vet was saying.

"Hose her down for the next forty-eight hours to reduce the inflammation," the vet continued, "and add a support bandage to the opposite leg. That should help it take the extra weight without becoming too strained."

"Well, that settles that then," Nick replied gloomily. "Feather isn't rideable for at least two months."

Tom sighed despondently. An injured horse was the last thing that Sandy Lane needed. Since Nick and Sarah had bought the stables three years ago, they had faced constant financial difficulties. It was hard enough already to compete with the more established stables in the area; every one of the horses needed to pull its weight if Sandy Lane was to survive. A horse eating tons of food and not working didn't bring in the money, even if the horse was very beautiful. And no one could dispute Feather's beauty. She was enchanting. A grey Arab with a coat so ghostly-white that she could have been mistaken for a phantom.

Tom knew that Feather wasn't really white, even if he liked to think she was. Everybody knew that there wasn't really such a thing as a white horse. On paper, they could be classified as light grey, iron grey, dappled grey or even flea-bitten grey... never white. Not one of the descriptions was right for Feather. Flea-bitten came the closest, for she had little black hairs over her coat giving her a slightly mottled appearance. But this struck Tom as a rather unflattering way to describe something as wonderful as a horse, especially a horse like Feather.

As Tom gazed across the stables, Feather looked out over her door. It was heartbreaking to see her confined to her stall. She was one of Nick and Sarah's most valuable animals and very popular with the older riders. There wasn't a horse at the stables to replace her.

Now where had Nick disappeared to? Tom thought to himself. Everywhere was deadly quiet this morning. Normally the hustle and bustle of the stables was well under way by now. Tom shrugged his shoulders. Nick must have gone to discuss things with Sarah at the house. Should he go and look for him there? He didn't want to disturb them, but at the same time he felt he would burst if he didn't tell someone his news.

The house lay to the left of the stables, near enough to be a part of it yet detached enough to be a separate home. Rambling wild roses covered the walls, hiding the crumbling brickwork. It was desperately in need of a lick of paint. Like everything at Sandy Lane it was slightly antiquated. Still Tom couldn't help feeling that both Nick and Sarah preferred it that way.

Both Nick and Sarah rode, although Sarah was

rarely in the stables nowadays. What with sorting out the mountain of bills and paperwork that kept flooding in, she simply didn't have the time. Nick however, couldn't be kept away from the horses. He'd been a jockey once upon a time, but had given it all up, vowed never to race again on the day that his steeplechaser, Golden Fleece, had fallen to her death. For a while, Sarah had thought that he would never even *ride* again, then they had bought Sandy Lane. Now Nick was trying to put the tragedy behind him.

Tom hurried over to the house and knocked on the back door. Nick and Sarah were deep in conversation as he walked into the kitchen, almost tripping over Ebony, the black Labrador who lay sprawled across the floor.

"I've been looking for you everywhere," Tom said.

"What's up?" Sarah asked, peering over her tortoiseshell glasses and looking intently at Tom. "I can't take any more bad news."

"No, no," said Tom. "It's good news actually."

"Well go on then. Fire away," Sarah said gloomily. "It'll make a change from all these figures."

"It's Georgina and Chancey you see," Tom started. "She's going away with her parents and she's left *me* to look after him... to do anything I want with. Isn't it the most fantastic news? She's not coming back for ages. Not for two and a half months... yippee. So I've got him all to myself and Horton Chancellor is ready to collect whenever I want." The words spilled out as Tom stopped to draw breath.

"Whoa, now slow down," said Sarah. "I can't understand a word you're saying. Who on earth are Georgina and Chancey and what is Horton Chancellor?"

"Sorry," said Tom, blushing furiously. "Georgina is

4

my awful cousin, Georgina Thompson, and Chancey is short for Horton Chancellor. You remember, the horse that took the showjumping circuit by storm last season when ridden by Emily Manners. He was bought for Georgina by my Uncle Bob," Tom added, beaming.

"Hmm. Let me think. Yes, I do remember that horse." Nick wrinkled up his forehead. "An absolute star... 15 hands, chestnut gelding, cleared everything in sight. Jumped like a dream if I remember rightly."

"That's the one," Tom replied. "Well, he's been loaned to me for the summer and I was wondering. Well, hoping really, that I might be able to keep him at Sandy Lane."

Nick and Sarah looked at each other. They knew what a chance this was for Tom, but it couldn't have come at a worse time for them. With Feather injured, they could ill-afford another horse, certainly not one that wasn't going to earn his keep. But Tom had been indispensable to them in the two years they had known him. How could they refuse his plea?

Sarah gazed fondly at Tom, remembering when he had first arrived at Sandy Lane, a shy, reserved eleven-year-old. How much he had changed since that day. He had told them then that he had wanted to ride for as long as he could remember. But his parents weren't horsy people and he had never been able to afford it. Then his Great Aunt Flo had died, leaving the family some money and his parents had thought it only fair that everyone should benefit. Tom, of course, had asked for the long-awaited riding lessons and been allowed to book twelve of them at Sandy Lane. Sarah had been touched by his story.

By the time the lessons were at an end, Tom was

totally hooked on riding and had started to spend more time than ever just helping out down at the stables. Nick and Sarah were more than happy to give him a free lesson in return for his work. Tom was to become the first of the helpers down at Sandy Lane – the regulars, as Nick and Sarah liked to call them. For that, they were especially attached to him. And there was no disputing his talent. He was a true horseman, born not made.

Nevertheless, an extra horse meant extra costs and Nick and Sarah had a business to run. Sarah also knew that Tom would never be able to afford a boarding fee and there was no way his mother would let him keep the horse in her prized flower garden.

"Stabling a horse isn't cheap Tom," Nick said thoughtfully. "You of all people know how much they cost and how much care they need."

"I know. I know all that. But school ends in two weeks, so I would be down here all summer anyway. I could give you my pocket money. I'd work extra hard... and... and..."

"We're not trying to be mean," Sarah went on. "It's just that now we've lost the use of Feather, that would make two horses eating and not paying their way."

"That's just it though," said Tom. "Horton Chancellor could pay his way. You could use him in lessons for the more experienced riders instead of Feather. I don't mind if it helps you out and I could ride him when he's not booked up. He wouldn't be any bother because I'd look after him."

Nick looked uncertain and sighed.

Tom took a deep breath.

"Well," Nick began hesitantly, "since you put it like

that." He smiled. Sarah raised her eyes to heaven. Tom knew that the battle was almost won.

"All right then," Nick finished. "Bring Chancey to Sandy Lane and we'll see how it goes."

"Thank you, oh thank you," Tom gasped. "I can't believe it. We won't let you down, I promise. Wait till I tell the others."

2

SANDY LANE FRIENDS

The others had been as excited as Tom when they heard his news. Alex, Kate, Jess and Rosie were all regulars at Sandy Lane. Of varying riding abilities, they all had two things in common – their passion for riding and their love of horses. In the week before Chancey's arrival, they could talk of little else but the prizewinning horse.

And Tom couldn't stop dreaming of the blissful days ahead of him. He was looking forward to a long summer filled with days upon days of riding. Tom told himself that he would work hard to become good enough to ride at Benbridge at the end of August – the show that everyone had set their hearts on. He could almost see it now... the breeze whipping past him as he flew around the course and rode through the finish to the sound of thunderous applause...

"That was Tom Buchanan on Horton Chancellor,

jumping clear with no time faults..."

Thud! Tom's vision was rudely interrupted as Napoleon kicked over his water bucket.

"Oh, you stupid animal. Look what you've done now," Tom said grumpily, as the water seeped across the floor of the stall. "I don't know. I'm always having to tidy up after you, aren't I?"

Automatically, Tom started to clean away the mess but his mind was elsewhere. He could barely contain his excitement. If someone had told him a month ago he would be loaned a horse for the whole summer, he would never have believed it. And Chancey was due to arrive tomorrow.

Walking across the stables, Tom refilled Napoleon's water bucket from the old trough. Water sprayed everywhere as he turned the faucets on full blast. He could see Rosie and Jess in the outdoor arena from where he was standing.

"Heels down, toes in, look straight ahead of you. What on earth has happened to the pair of you?" Nick bellowed. "Your hands and forearms should form a straight line with the reins. If you're not going to concentrate, Jess, you may as well not be here."

Rosie and Jess were in the same year at school... best of friends and yet complete opposites. Where Rosie was careful, quiet and rational, Jess was impulsive, daring... and often in trouble.

As their lesson came to an end, the two best friends wandered into the stables, chattering loudly. Quickly tethering their ponies to the rails, they started sponging them down.

"Hey," cried Rosie, as Jess dipped her body brush into the bucket and doused her with water. "We're supposed to be grooming the ponies, not each other."

"Well, I've been trying to attract your attention for ages," laughed Jess. "I've been splashing you for the last five minutes and you've only just noticed. You must have gone over Pepper's withers at least a dozen times. You'll rub him away if you're not careful."

Tom wandered away, smiling to himself. He was small for his thirteen years with tousled brown hair and a round, cheerful face. As the star pupil at Sandy Lane, he could have been arrogant and impossible, yet he wasn't. Always willing to help with whatever needed to be done, Tom was well-liked. There was no horse he couldn't handle, or so Jess and Rosie thought. They secretly admired him and hoped that one day they would be as good as him.

"Jess, have you got time to tack up Napoleon?" Tom called from the tack room. "I've got to get Hector ready, and then I think Nick is just about set to take the 4 o'clock class."

"Sure," said Jess. "Rosie, can you keep an eye on Minstrel for me? I'll be back in a minute."

Quickly, Jess slipped into Napoleon's box. Slipping the halter down the bay neck, she put the bridle on. She was a real hand at tacking up now. Still she hadn't always found it that easy. Many tears of frustration had been shed when she was still learning the basics. Now however, without hesitation, she slid the saddle smoothly down Napoleon's back and tightened the girth. Heading out into the blazing sunshine, she took him to the mounting block as Tom led out Hector.

Hector was a big sturdy bay hack, with a coat of polished mahogany, that Sarah had inherited from a woman looking for a good home for him. He was

Alex's favorite at the stables, and everyone was very fond of him. He was twenty years old – an old man in horse years – but a solid ride and ideal for beginners. He was the first horse that Tom had ever ridden and at 16 hands, Tom had felt as small as a sparrow on top of an elephant!

Soon everyone was mounted and the ride was ready. As Nick led the class out of the stables, Tom thought how tired he looked. He hoped that Nick and Sarah would have more luck this year. Sandy Lane was such a fantastic stables, it seemed so unfair that they were continually struggling. As Tom walked back into the stables, he saw the last two of his friends arrive.

"Aha! Alex, Kate, you're here at last, you lazy sloths," he yelled. Alex and Kate were brother and sister and usually went everywhere as a pair.

"Ugh. We were forced to go to our Aunt June's fortieth birthday party," groaned Alex. "Total nightmare. All our relatives telling us how much we'd grown. We got here as quickly as we could. Hopefully we won't have to do any more family gatherings for a while, not till Christmas anyway."

"Well, you've arrived right on time to help turn out the horses for the evening anyway."

"Great," Alex groaned, lazily. "Is that all you've got to say to me? I haven't seen my best friend for a couple of days and he puts me to work straight away."

"There's a lot to be done and I am supposed to be coming over to your house later anyway," said Tom, grinning.

"Well, what's the news on Chancey?" Alex asked.

"He's arriving tomorrow at eleven, so make sure you're here to greet him," Tom said, looking around him at his friends. "Personally, I don't know how I'll ever get to sleep tonight. Come on Alex," he said, turning to his friend. "I'll help you turn out those horses..."

3

A BAD BEGINNING

Tom did manage to get to sleep and woke early the next morning. Too early. By seven, he'd been awake for what seemed like ages and could stand it no longer. Getting out of bed, he walked over to the window and looked outside. He smiled. It was going to be a very sunny day.

Pulling on his jeans, Tom hurried down the stairs and strode out into the morning air. Narrowly escaping his mother's breakfast call, he set off for the stables. It was a good fifteen minute bicycle ride to Sandy Lane from where Tom lived, on the outskirts of nearby Colcott, but one that he didn't mind too much. Whistling to himself as he passed the old tannery, he sped down the hill.

Not far now. Out of breath as he reached the last stretch, he zoomed past the duck pond at the corner of the stables and hurtled into the yard. The horses had already been brought in from the fields and the stables were buzzing with activity.

"Tom, throw me a dandy brush will you?" Jess called. She was going to have her work cut out grooming Minstrel. He was a skewbald and the white parts of him got extremely muddy. Tom handed her the dandy brush and headed off to make a start on Napoleon. Cheerfully, they chatted together as they busied themselves around the stables.

By a quarter to eleven, Nick had taken two classes and a hack. The day was fully under way. As usual, Alex and Kate were late and didn't get to the stables until five to eleven, when most of the work had already been done. As they arrived, an approaching engine could be heard rounding the corner to Sandy Lane and they had to jump out of the way as a large horse van ground to a halt beside them. This was the moment everyone had been waiting for. Chancey had arrived.

Everyone was quiet as a disgruntled-looking man stepped down from the cab, alone.

Where's Georgina? Tom thought to himself. Surely she would have come with Chancey to settle him in and say goodbye.

"I don't know what you've got in there," said the man, hunching his shoulders. "Supposed to be a horse... well, he was when I loaded him anyway. A real handful. Only just managed to get him in the van and that was nothing compared to the ride here. Thought he was going to kick the van down. Better you than me, son," he said, climbing into the van before Tom had a chance to reply.

There was a frantic whinny and the sound of drumming hooves reverberated around the stables as

Chancey pranced down the ramp. He was certainly on his toes, but he didn't look like the sleek, well turned-out horse that Tom remembered seeing last season. He was still unclipped and his shabby winter coat was flecked with foam, as feverishly he pawed the ground. No one knew what to say.

Eventually, Rosie managed to pipe up with: "Are you sure it's the same horse?"

"Of course it is," Tom snapped, unable to keep the disappointment out of his voice. "He only needs to be clipped and he'll look fine."

"I wouldn't be so sure," Jess muttered under her breath.

"Shouldn't he have been clipped already?" said Rosie. She was always looking things up in her Pony Club manual and was sure that she had read that horses should be clipped before January, or their summer coat would be spoiled.

"He probably should have been, still that won't be too much of a problem," said Nick kindly. "Now come on everyone, stop crowding him and get back to what you were doing. Take him to his new home, Tom."

Tom approached the horse and took the halter that the man offered him. Chancey jumped skittishly from side to side, rolling his eyes and flicking his tail as Tom led him off.

"Poor Tom," said Rosie. "He was so excited about that horse. Still, even though Chancey isn't very good-looking, I'm sure he'll be an absolute dream to ride."

Tom didn't know what to think. When he had seen Chancey last season, he had been one hundred percent fit, his muscles rippling under his glossy chestnut coat. Tom was sure that he hadn't been mistaken, he was definitely the same horse.

Tom picked up the things that the van driver had left in the middle of the stables. There was a saddle and bridle, a dark blue New Zealand blanket and a box full of glossy grooming brushes that looked as though they had never been used. Putting them in the tack room, he grabbed an old body brush and curry comb, and hurried back to Chancey's stall. He would have to be quick if he was going to be able to give Chancey a quick grooming and get home in time for lunch. Tom opened the door slowly, careful not to startle him.

"Come on, boy. Let's get you cleaned up and give you your lunch. I bet you're hungry after that awful trip," he crooned.

Chancey seemed to have settled down a little and nuzzled Tom's pockets inquisitively. Tom fumbled around for a mint. The horse's lips were as soft as crushed velvet as he gratefully accepted the offering.

"That's better," said Tom. "I thought you'd taken an instant dislike to me, and it's very important that we're friends if we're going to spend the whole summer together."

"Hey, now hang on a minute," said Tom, as the nuzzling turned into a frantic chewing. "I'm sure my jacket doesn't taste that great and I won't be getting a new one if you eat it either." Gently, Tom pushed Chancey's nose away.

"I've got to go home for lunch in a minute," Tom went on, giving him a quick rubdown. "I'll be back at two. Nick has said that we can join the 3 o'clock class. Are you listening?"

Chancey wasn't paying any notice. Already bored

of all the attention, his head was buried deep in a bucket of pony pellets as Tom bolted the door of the stall and set off for home.

Lunch was something that Tom's mother insisted upon. If he was going to be at the stables all day, she said that he must at least come back at one to eat. He was careful to obey her, if only to stop her from going on about the amount of time he spent at Sandy Lane.

It was already ten to one. He was going to be late again. Great. He would have to get going, and fast.

Tom got home at five past one. Rushing inside, he headed straight for the bathroom to wash his hands. The rest of his family were already starting lunch when Tom stumbled to the table and sat himself down before anything could be said. His little sister, Sophie, was reading.

"Put that away, Sophie," her mother said sternly. "How many times do I have to tell you it's rude to read at the table?"

"Well, Dad does it," Sophie answered back. "He's always reading the paper and eating at the same time."

"Well, that's different. When you're your father's age, you'll be allowed to do it too," she said, as Sophie surreptitiously slid the book onto her lap.

"Come on David, we really ought to set an example to the children," said Mrs. Buchanan, turning to her husband. Tom's father looked up from his paper.

"So, how was cousin Georgina then?" he asked Tom as he put away his paper. "Did you remember to thank her for lending you her horse?"

"Well, the strange thing is, she didn't come with Chancey," said Tom. "He was delivered by a stranger."

"What's so strange about that?" asked his mother.

"Perhaps Georgina has got too much to do before she goes away. Packing can be a nightmare. It always takes me ages."

Tom shrugged his shoulders. He wasn't convinced that was the reason. If he was ever lucky enough to own his own horse, he knew he would simply make time to say goodbye. He didn't think he would even be able to leave his horse's side... not for a whole summer.

"What's the horse like though?" asked Sophie, looking up from her lap.

"OK," said Tom.

"Just OK?" said Mr. Buchanan. "But we've heard of nothing other than this horse for the last week. He must be better than OK."

"He will be, but I haven't tried him yet," Tom said tiredly. He didn't want to tell them how Chancey had come careening out of the horse van – his mother would only worry.

Tom might have been having lunch with his family, but his mind was elsewhere.

"Oh Thomas, you haven't gulped down your food have you? You'll get indigestion if you're not careful."

Tom's mother only called him Thomas when she was really annoyed with him.

"Sorry," said Tom. "But I do have to get back to Sandy Lane. Nick has said that I can ride Chancey in the 3 o'clock class. May I get down from the table?"

"Hmm. All right then," said Mrs. Buchanan. "You mustn't be back late though. It isn't the summer break yet. You still have your homework to do..." Her voice trailed off as Tom dove for his riding hat and shot to the door.

"Thanks Mom," he said.

Tom scooted out of the house and threw himself onto his bike. The countryside sped past as he raced off to Sandy Lane. He hardly even noticed the uphill climb on the way back, and soon he was pedaling into the stable grounds.

Scrambling off his bike, he went to find Nick. He didn't have to look far. Nick was sitting at the desk in the tack room, signing people in for the next ride and collecting the money.

"Who's in the 3 o'clock, Nick?" Tom asked.

"Anna, Mark, Claudine, Lydia and... someone I don't remember... oh, could it be you?" Nick smiled teasingly.

"Phew!" Tom gasped. They were all pretty good riders. He hoped that he was up to it, that he wouldn't let Chancey down.

"Do you want to go and tack up Chancey then, Tom? He seems to have settled in all right now. And we're almost ready to start."

"Sure," Tom smiled, hurrying off.

As he let himself into the stall, Chancey's brown face turned to look at him inquiringly. Tom patted his neck and tickled his nose, letting the horse smell his clothes to get used to him. Then, deftly, he tacked him up and led him out of his stall, down the lane and into the outdoor arena. Rosie, Jess, Alex and Kate gathered to watch.

"He looks much better now that he's been groomed and rested," said Rosie.

"Yes, and he doesn't have that crazy glint in his eye anymore," said Jess encouragingly. "He was probably just a little unsettled by the van ride."

1 9

Tom felt proud as he walked around the ring and thought back to how well Chancey had performed on the circuit last season. He knew that he was on a good horse and trembled with anticipation at the power beneath him.

Chancey arched his neck and let out a loud whinny. He was well proportioned, with shoulders that sloped smoothly up to his withers and wide, muscular flanks.

"Is this the new horse that you were telling us about Nick?" asked Anna. She normally rode Feather, but since the little mare had gone lame, had been riding Hector and was looking for a smaller replacement.

"Yes," said Nick. "As I said, he's Tom's, but other people will be able to ride him if they like."

Loosening up their horses, the riders started at a posting trot and then, one by one, began to canter around the track. Chancey wanted to take the lead and Tom found it hard to keep him behind the others.

"Can you all return to a walk and shorten your stirrups. We're going to try some jumping," Nick called, sending everybody off to the other end of the ring.

They were going to start with a pair of cross poles and jump from a trot. Anna trotted Hector around, and took him neatly over the jump, as did the other riders. Tom watched intently as Mark took off too early with Jester. Tom felt uneasy as Chancey jogged on the spot, fighting for his head.

"Mark, I'll put a pole on the ground in front of the jump to mark the takeoff and then you can try it again," Nick called from the middle of the ring. This time, Jester jumped successfully.

Looking back, Tom couldn't remember when it all

began to go so desperately wrong. Chancey had already started shying at imaginary creatures in the hedgerow and Tom was finding it increasingly difficult to hold him. As the pair approached the jump, Chancey threw his head in the air and dashed toward it.

"Try not to check him too much Tom," Nick shouted. "I know it's hard, but he's fighting with you for control. If you try to alter his strides, he's going to lose his balance."

Tom and Chancey headed for the jump. With a loud snort and a flash of his tail, Chancey ducked out from the jump and swerved to the right. And then he was off, charging around the ring. Three circuits later, an ashen-faced Tom had managed to pull him up.

"Right Tom," Nick called. "I think that's enough excitement for one day."

"That horse looks crazy," said Anna. " He's certainly not another Feather."

Nick stared silently. "Tom, don't worry, I'll talk to you about it later."

It was easy for Nick to sound confident, but Tom knew Anna was right. Chancey had looked crazy, and Nick had been counting on being able to use him as a replacement for Feather.

Back in Chancey's stall, Tom started to untack the horse. He ran the stirrups up the leathers on the saddle before sliding it off. Then, in a trance, he slipped the strap of the halter over the chestnut neck and took off the bridle.

"Why, oh why, did you have to make me look like that?" he sighed, burying his head in Chancey's mane. "You totally humiliated me and in front of everyone... all of my friends at Sandy Lane. No one will want to ride you now, and then what will happen? It's only because of Nick and Sarah's kindness that you're here anyway. You were supposed to be looking after me today."

Chancey stared balefully at Tom. There was not a hint of apology in his dark eyes.

"I'm not going to cry," Tom said through gritted teeth. "I'm not going to let you win. I know how good you can be. I've seen how good you can be. I'm going to make you that good again. I'm going to take you to the top. I swear it."

4

BACK TO SQUARE ONE

It was dark when Tom got home. His parents had been starting to worry. But when he pushed open the back door and walked headlong into his mother, she could see he was upset and let him skip supper.

Alone in his room, he sat down on his bed and let out a loud sigh. It was so easy to feel determined about Chancey at Sandy Lane, but when he was away from the stables, doubts crowded his mind. He looked around his room. Every wall was covered with posters of horses and famous riders – riders on whom he had modeled himself. How stupid he had been. What had made him think he could ever be as good as any of them? He simply didn't have it in him.

"It was me who was at fault today, not Chancey," he said aloud. "If I was any good, I would have been able to control him."

Despondently, he put his head in his hands. What

should he do? Clearly the horse wasn't suitable for lessons and he couldn't really expect Nick and Sarah to keep Chancey on at Sandy Lane for free.

At the same time, Nick and Sarah were talking along similar lines in the house at Sandy Lane.

"We've got to be realistic. We can't use himfor lessons. What if he went crazy with one of our clients? It would ruin our reputation," said Sarah.

"You're right," Nick said glumly.

"We'll have to buy another horse to replace Feather. You'll need to tell Tom that he can't keep Chancey with us any more," said Sarah.

"What!" said Nick. "We can't do that, Sarah. You know that Tom has set his heart on having him."

"Still, we only agreed to it on the understanding that we would be able to use the horse in lessons," said Sarah, "and now that's clearly impossible. It was bad enough supporting one horse that wasn't pulling its weight but *two*."

Nick looked downcast. "But Chancey is a magnificent animal. If we can get him back to his old self, we could use him in lessons. And if he's seen performing well at shows, it'll do Sandy Lane's reputation no end of good."

"What if we can't?" Sarah had put Nick's worst fears into words. "He's obviously been ruined somewhere along the line. Oh, if only you weren't so impetuous, Nick Brooks."

"Well, if it comes to it, I suppose we could sell Whispering Silver," Nick said tentatively. "We'd get a good price for her. She'd make an excellent hunter and then we could afford to buy a replacement for Feather and have some money left over to buy another horse too."

Sarah gazed at him fondly. He really meant it. He was willing to give up the horse he valued most in the world – Whispering Silver, the retired racehorse he had nursed back to health. No one else had thought that Nick could do it. Sarah thought back to the day he had bought her at the sale, saving her from the glue factory. It had turned out all right in the end, but for a while it had been touch and go as to whether she would even live.

"No, Nick. I don't want you to do that. You need Whisp to take lessons on," Sarah continued, breaking the silence. "Besides, she's yours. She couldn't possibly belong to anyone else. You were the one who saved her life." Sarah took a deep breath. "No, we'll find the extra money somehow. If we start scouting through the horse magazines we'll get something, only we won't be able to aim as high as Feather."

"But horses are so much more expensive if you buy them privately. Couldn't we..."

"No, Nick," groaned Sarah. "Promise me one thing... no more sales. It's too much of a risk. You just don't know what you're going to end up with. We want guarantees, vets' certificates... no more gambles."

"You're right. I know you're right," said Nick.

Sarah smiled.

"Now, are you going to be the one to tell Tom of our decision?" she asked quietly.

"Yes, I'll go and have a talk with him now."

"Now?" said Sarah, looking at her watch. "But Mrs. Buchanan will freak. It's so late to turn up on someone's doorstep uninvited."

"I know. But this can't wait until the morning. He

was so disappointed."

"OK," said Sarah. "And make sure you agree on some sort of training program..."

Sarah didn't have a chance to finish her sentence as Nick hurried out of the house and climbed into their battered old Bronco. Revving up the engine, he headed out of Sandy Lane. Tom lived in a new housing development about four miles away. It was as far removed from the world of Sandy Lane as you could get – neat paths, manicured lawns, clipped hedges. Nick couldn't imagine Tom being allowed in the kitchen in his dirty riding boots.

Even though Mrs. Buchanan was surprised to see Nick when she opened the door, she didn't ask any questions. She knew Tom was upset but was careful not to pry into his other world.

"Tom, you have a visitor," she called up the stairs.

Tom looked up as Nick stuck his head around the door.

"Can I come in, Tom?" he asked gently. Tom nodded. He knew what Nick had come to say, knew that it was unfair of him to expect otherwise. After all, Nick and Sarah did have a business to run.

"Don't say anything. You don't have to explain. I know he's no use." Tom blurted out the words.

"Hey, now hold on a minute," said Nick looking surprised. "I didn't come here to say that." He smiled.

"I know things this afternoon weren't that great. But it's not the end of the world. Chancey was and could still be a champion. We can't use him in lessons at the moment, and Sarah and I will have to think about buying a horse to replace Feather..."

"I know and I'm so sorry, Nick," Tom interrupted.

"Hang on," said Nick. "That's not for you to worry about. It's our problem." Tom listened desperately as Nick continued.

"Sarah and I have decided to take a chance with the horse, if you'll excuse the pun," he grinned. "If you're prepared to put in the work, we'll let you keep him on at the stables. What do you say?"

"Oh yes," Tom breathed, hardly able to believe what he was hearing.

"Right. Well, first things first," said Nick. "We'll have to take him back to the beginning and train him again. I don't want to guess what your cousin's been doing with him. All I know is that if Chancey was once a champion, which he clearly was, then he can be made a champion again. We've got just under eight weeks if he's to be fit and ready for the Benbridge show at the end of August," Nick finished. "Do you want to take on the challenge?"

"You bet," said Tom, grinning from under the strand of hair that had fallen over his face. "What do you want me to do?"

"Well, he'll have to be clipped. I'll organize that this week while you're at school. And he'll need to be shod and have his teeth checked. They'll probably have to be floated. Then we'll have to discuss a schedule for training and getting him in shape, and carefully monitor his eating habits."

"I can do that," said Tom, eagerly.

"I'm not going to have a great deal of time to help you right away. There's a lot going on at Sandy Lane at the moment, so you must be patient," Nick continued. "Oh and most important of all. You must swear that you won't take Chancey out on your own.

Not until I think you're both ready for it anyway. We just can't trust him at the moment. He's dangerous. Sarah would never forgive me if anything was to happen to you," he chuckled. "Besides, I don't want people thinking we're not safe at Sandy Lane. So, do I have your word?"

"Of course, Nick. I promise."

"Well, that's about it then. You could come down to Sandy Lane after school on Wednesday if you like. I should have had a chance to do a little work with him by then. I've got a spare hour at five. We could spend it in the ring. What do you say?"

"Fantastic." Tom beamed.

"When does the school year end by the way?" asked Nick.

"Next Friday," Tom answered.

"Good," said Nick. "Well, see you Wednesday evening then."

It was a statement rather than a question. Everything had been decided so quickly. Tom looked up half-embarrassed.

"Will you thank Sarah for me? And, I... I... well... thank you."

Nick smiled and closed the door behind him.

* * * * * * * * * * * * * * *

Time went so slowly over the next three days. Tom could hardly believe it when on Wednesday the bell sounded around the school as the day ended. He was the first to get to the classroom door and bolted out of the building before anyone could stop him.

"Another day over, two more to go," he chanted to himself.

Turning out of the school drive, Tom sprinted to the stables. When he reached Sandy Lane, Tom hurried straight to the outdoor arena. Nick was as good as his word and already had Chancey on a longe line. The saddle on Chancey's back looked funny without any stirrups. As he trotted around the arena, he looked altogether like a different horse. He was calm for one thing.

"I've been longeing him since Monday. He's been getting better and better. Come into the middle here," said Nick, clicking Chancey on into a canter, flicking the whip lightly toward his hock. "He hasn't forgotten his gaits."

Nick slowed Chancey down to a trot with the word 'ter-rot'. Tom walked into the arena and took the longe line that Nick offered him. Nick stood next to Tom and guided him through the horse's gaits. Tom only needed to use the whip very lightly as Chancey started to respond to the sound of his voice.

"Very good," said Nick. "Let's try him with some loose jumping. I think Georgina must have been fighting with him for control before a jump, that's why he's so nervous. Every horse likes to find his own natural takeoff point." Nick put up some cross poles and got Tom to longe Chancey over them.

"You see. He jumps perfectly on his own. And because the poles are crossed, it gets him to take off in the middle of the jump. Give him another five minutes

29

and then we'll put him away for the night," said Nick.

"He's been so well behaved. I don't think we want to push him too hard. We could try taking him out this weekend. It's just a matter of building up mutual trust. He's not really a problem horse and he's certainly not too old to learn..." Nick's voice trailed off as the ring of the telephone sounded from the tack room.

"Oh darn," Nick said. "I'll speak to you later," he called, running for the phone.

"You see, there's hope for you yet," Tom said, turning to lead Chancey up the drive. "Now, you listen here. I won't see you for a while now. Well, not until Saturday anyway, so you'd better be on your best behavior."

The stables were still as Tom and Chancey crunched across the gravel. Tom led the horse to his stall and gave him a quick rubdown. Tenderly, he pulled Chancey's ears before bolting him in for the night. Slinging the bridle over his shoulder and carrying the saddle on his arm, he crossed the stables to return them to the tack room.

"How would you like going to the Ash Hill horse sale with me on Saturday morning, Tom?" Nick's voiced echoed around the stables. "Just to have a look around."

"Isn't Sarah always telling us how risky it is to buy at a sale?" Tom called back, confused. But Nick was out of earshot and there was no reply. Tom shrugged his shoulders. He knew he should be pleased that out of everyone, Nick had asked him to go with him. But he couldn't help feeling that it would be a waste of time and he had really wanted to ride Chancey on

Saturday morning. Oh well, perhaps they could do some work with him in the afternoon.

Tom shivered as he strolled over to his bike and headed off into the still evening. He was exhausted, but at last he felt he was getting somewhere with Chancey. It had been a long day, and yet one that marked a turning point for Tom... one he wouldn't forget in a hurry.

5

STORM CLOUD

Saturday arrived quicker than Tom could have imagined. Rolling over in bed, he looked out of the window and smiled. He would be able to spend the whole day with Chancey. Then he groaned... the Ash Hill sale – and he'd said to Nick that he would go with him. He'd have to get a move on, it started at nine. Hurriedly, he threw on some clothes, grabbed a slice of bread and rushed outside to his bike.

He got to the bottom of Clee Hill in record time and pedaled hard to the top. Taking his feet out of the pedals as he reached the summit, he zoomed down the other side and into Sandy Lane. Nick was already waiting when Tom reached the stables.

"All set Tom?" he smiled. "Now, we'll just look at the horses that are fully guaranteed. I want to see what's around at the moment but we're not going to buy anything."

"Well, shouldn't we take the horse van just in case?" Tom asked.

"No," said Nick rather too quickly. "If we don't take it, we won't be tempted."

Tom smiled to himself. He'd heard it all before. If Nick got carried away, nothing would stop him from being tempted.

Jumping into the Bronco, they jolted out of the stables, down Sandy Lane and onto the road to Ash Hill. The engine groaned as Nick changed gear and they chugged along. It didn't take them long to drive the two miles.

Tom frowned as he got out at the sale and stared in despair at the long rows of horses. It was the most depressing place on earth. Why had he agreed to come? All of these horses and ponies – creatures from good homes and once well-loved, now standing alone awaiting their fate.

"Have a look at the catalog, Tom. I've marked a couple of possibles."

Tom looked at the entries Nick had put an x by – a registered bay mare of 14.2 hands, and a grey hunter.

"What about this one too, Nick?" Tom asked, pointing to a lot in the catalog.

"Registered yellow dun working pony, four-year-old, two white socks, 13.2 hands without shoes. Fully guaranteed. Sounds good," Nick said.

"Come on, let's go and have a look."

But they didn't get that far. As they made their way down the lines of horses, Tom could see that Nick's eye was immediately caught by a fragile, dappled-grey pony in the corner. Tied to a muddy piece of rope, her head downcast, she didn't even look up as they

33

approached. She was so thin. Tom knew from that moment that Nick was caught. He couldn't bear to drag himself away from the little pony. Gently Nick stroked her shoulder as she tilted her delicately dished face toward him, nuzzling his pockets for tidbits. Quickly, he ran his hands down her legs.

"There isn't time to see her run up in hand. Look at the welts in her coat, Tom. She's been badly neglected. And she can't be any older than three. Her conformation is good."

And then they heard the bidding start.

"Come on, let's hurry," said Nick.

Swiftly, they made their way to the ringside. Nick turned to his catalog.

"Lot number one, what will you give me for this bay cob here?" the auctioneer was saying.

"Who'll start me at three hundred? Three hundred. Am I bid three fifty? Three fifty, I'm bid. Four hundred?"

It was all happening so quickly, that Tom could hardly make out what was going on. Before he knew it, the cob had been sold to a man at the back.

"Glue factory," said Nick. Tom felt tears well up in his eyes and blinked them away. He was going to have to be much tougher. If only he was rich, he would buy them all. He turned away, wanting to be apart from it.

"There are only ten more lots and then she's in," Nick whispered. "Probably about fifteen minutes if you want to go and grab a lemonade," he said, seeing Tom's pale face.

"I think that might be a good idea," Tom smiled weakly.

Tom squeezed through the crowd and headed for

the refreshments tent. Joining the line of people milling around, he felt as though he wasn't quite a part of it – like watching some sort of pantomime.

As he made his way back to Nick, he realized that the little grey pony was being led around the ring and Nick was in the bidding.

"I'll just go fifty more," Nick whispered as he raised his card in the air.

There was a deathly hush. Tom took a deep breath, praying that no one else would bid.

"Any advance on four hundred? Will anyone give me four fifty? All done at four hundred?" the auctioneer was saying.

Tom held his breath in anticipation.

"Four hundred I'm bid once. Four hundred twice. Going... going... gone."

With that the auctioneer banged his hammer on the desk.

"Sold to the man at the back," he said, staring straight at Nick. Tom turned to Nick and grinned. They had got her.

"Name?" he called.

"Nick Brooks," Nick answered.

"Address?" the man returned.

"Sandy Lane Stables, Sandy Lane, near Colcott."

It was all over, and without a second's thought, the auctioneer had turned his attention to the next lot.

"You have to pay in advance," a voice called from behind a counter at the side of the ring. Tom glanced over to see a woman sitting at a desk, looking out of place in a blue sweater with bright red nail polish.

"I know," said Nick, reaching for his wallet.

Once they had paid and collected the relevant

papers, Tom and Nick made their way over to where the little grey pony had been left. Quickly, Nick untethered her, talking to her all the time in a soft voice.

"We'll soon have you away from here my girl," he soothed.

"What's she called?" Tom asked quietly.

"Storm Cloud," Nick answered.

"Storm Cloud," Tom breathed. "It's perfect for her," he said, as the three of them walked slowly away from the sale.

"Why don't you hop up on her and I'll lead," Nick said quickly. "We'll come back later for the Bronco."

"OK," said Tom, bending his knee for Nick to give him a leg-up. "What's Sarah going to say?"

"Well," Nick reddened, "that's not for you to worry about. I don't think she'll be too delighted, but when she sees Storm Cloud she'll feel differently. Sarah might pretend to be as hard as nails, but underneath it all, she's a softy."

"Well, at least Storm Cloud's fully guaranteed," said Tom. "That's one thing, so you won't have to pay any vet's bills. Fingers crossed. "

Slowly, they picked their way along the grass verge by the side of the road.

"She's got a nice long stride," Tom continued. "She just seems a little tired."

"Oh, she only needs fattening up," said Nick. "There's plenty of summer grass for her to chow down on at home."

They walked along in silent contemplation as the traffic sped past. Storm Cloud didn't even flinch at the cars.

"Could we do some training with Chancey this

afternoon, Nick?" Tom asked, breaking the silence.

"I don't see why not. Sarah's taking out the trail riders," he answered. "It'll be a good opportunity for us to get started with him."

"Great," said Tom, as Nick pulled Storm Cloud's head up from the grass.

"Come on. You'll have enough of that later," he said, "but we've got to get you home first and we're almost there."

Tom wrinkled up his nose as they passed the pig farm and neared the stables. They passed Bucknell Woods and were at the bottom of the drive in no time at all. Slowly, they strolled into the stables.

"Tom, do you think you could take care of Storm Cloud for me?" said Nick. "Put her in the stall by the tack room. I'd better go and tell Sarah about our latest acquisition," he said sheepishly.

"Sure," said Tom, jumping swiftly to the ground. "Come on, Stormy," he whispered, as he led her to the stall. She was sweating slightly, tired after the long walk home. Tom rubbed her shivering body with a wisp of straw.

Moments later, Nick appeared with Sarah. Tom led Storm Cloud out and circled her as a group gathered to see the latest addition, waiting to hear if she was given the Sandy Lane seal of approval. Quickly, Sarah ran her hands down the horse's legs.

"Well, she's sound, and she's got kind eyes, even if she doesn't look in great shape." She patted her on the shoulder. "She'll soon fill out," she smiled, turning to Nick, "even if she was from a sale." Everyone breathed a sigh of relief. Sarah did know her stuff.

"Come on Tom," said Nick as everyone dispersed.

"Come and help, and then we could take Chancey out for that ride I promised you."

"Well, if you think he's ready for it," Tom stammered nervously.

"He'll be all right if we take it slowly," said Nick.

Tom hurried off to prepare a quick bran mash for Storm Cloud as Nick led the dejected horse back to her new home. It didn't take them long to get her blanketed and give her a quick rubdown. And then Tom rushed to get Chancey ready. Feeling guilty that his beloved horse had taken a back seat, so enthralled had he been with the dappled grey pony, Tom was determined to do an extra good job of grooming him.

And sure enough, Tom didn't rest content until he could have sworn he saw his reflection in Chancey's coat. Putting the bit into the horse's mouth, Tom slipped the bridle on and fastened the throat latch. Carefully, he slid the saddle down Chancey's back and tightened the girth. Adjusting his riding hat, he led the horse out of his stall.

"Wow," said Nick. "Tom, you've done an amazing job on him. Chancey looks wonderful."

Tom glowed at Nick's words of praise. Climbing into their saddles, they strolled out of the stables and through the gate at the back. Tom hummed happily to himself. Neither of them said a word as they lengthened their reins and rode across the fields. It was a beautiful July day, the aquamarine sky was intense and the smell of the country engulfed them. Chancey's coat shone a burnished red as the sun beat down on their backs and they entered Larkfield Copse. Tom didn't think he could ever feel happier, certainly never as content, as he lost himself in his riding and he and his horse became as one. And suddenly, they were out of the trees and crossing the old coastal track, over to the open fields that led to the cliff tops. Tom could smell the salt in the air. Chancey snorted excitedly, swishing his tail with a determined air.

"Come on, let's have a canter," Nick said mischievously. "Make sure you stay behind me and try to let me go for a few strides before you let Chancey follow. I don't want you forcing me into a gallop," he laughed. "Luckily Whisp won't panic – she's too much of an old lady for that. She'll hold you back."

Tom crouched low in the saddle and urged Chancey on after Nick. They rode like the wind and, as they pounded across the springy turf, it seemed as though they were covering miles. All at once, there was a fallen tree in their path. For a moment, Tom was startled. What would Chancey do? They were going at quite a speed. And then he remembered all that Nick had told him – let the horse do the work and don't interfere. Scornfully, Chancey soared three feet above the log. Nick looked under his arm in amazement, as he slowed down to a trot and then to a walk.

"That was magnificent Tom," he said breathlessly. "He jumps like a deer. I haven't seen a horse like him in a long time."

Tom smiled to himself as they made their way back to the stables. Winding their way through the little copse of trees, they let their horses stretch their heads after their exertions. Slowly ambling back the way that they had come less than an hour ago, they picked their way through the fields, back through the gate to Sandy Lane and clattered noisily into the stable grounds.

6

TOM'S SECRET

It was a wet, muggy, Wednesday morning. Tom was fed up as he sat in the tack room watching the summer rain splatter down the window pane. Chancey hadn't been ridden for well over a week.

Pitter... patter... pitter... patter. The rain hammered rhythmically against the outside of the building. Tracing patterns in the condensation, Tom outlined the horse's head that he had become so good at drawing.

Nick hurried in out of the rain, holding his waterproof jacket over his head as an umbrella. He had been caught in the summer shower unawares and the tack room had been his nearest shelter.

"I've been longeing Storm Cloud. She's got so much potential. If she continues the way she's going, it won't be long before I'll be able to use her in lessons," Nick said proudly. "What's up with you?" he asked, seeing Tom's glum face.

"Oh, nothing really. I was just wondering if you might have some time to look at Chancey and me today?" Tom said quietly.

"Not today, Tom. I haven't got a spare moment," Nick answered. "I'm giving two classes, maybe even three and then I really need to do another hour with Storm Cloud. You could lead him around the ring for half an hour if you like."

"Couldn't I ride Chancey with the trail class, Nick?" Tom pleaded.

"I don't think it's a very good idea, Tom. He's not ready for it yet. You know how agitated he gets if he's with more than one horse. He tried to kick Jester last time he was out."

Tom sighed impatiently. He knew what Nick was saying was true, but at this rate, Chancey was never going to be ready for the Benbridge show. He felt mean complaining. Nick and Sarah had done so much for him. If it wasn't for them, he wouldn't even have had a home for the horse. Nevertheless, Chancey did need to be trained if he was going to get in shape. And if Nick didn't have the time to help, there wasn't a great deal that Tom could do about it. Or was there?

And suddenly it came to him. Perhaps he could do something to help. Perhaps *he* could train Chancey. Nick didn't need to know anything about it. After all, Chancey had gone so well for him the last time he had ridden him and he hadn't really needed Nick there, had he?

Tom sighed. He knew that it wasn't quite true. He did need Nick, and Nick had expressly forbidden him to take Chancey out on his own.

Tom put his head around the tack room door and

stepped outside. He held out his hands. It was still pouring as he crossed the stable grounds to Chancey's stall.

"If I got up early in the mornings and trained you, nobody would even notice," Tom whispered, trying to convince himself as much as Chancey that he wouldn't be doing anything wrong.

"You'd like that too," he murmured. "You'd get out more then. We'd have to be very careful that we weren't caught, that's all."

Chancey snorted, as if in response, a piece of straw hanging from his mouth.

"You shouldn't be chewing on that either," said Tom crossly. "If you eat too much of it, you'll find you end up with colic."

That was what made Tom's mind up. If Chancey was eating his bed, he must be more bored than Tom had imagined.

"We'll start training tomorrow, then. I'll get here early to tack you up."

"What are you doing in there, Tom?" asked Alex, poking his head over the stall door. "You're not talking to yourself are you?"

"No," said Tom, turning bright red. "Just Chancey."

"You're crazy!" Alex chuckled. "What are you saying to him anyway?"

The thought of letting Alex in on his plans passed fleetingly through Tom's mind. He opened his mouth to tell him, and then closed it firmly again. No, it wasn't fair. It wasn't fair to expect Alex to lie for him. This was something he had decided to undertake. He had to bear the full responsibility.

"Are you reading me?" said Alex. "Come in Tom.

Are you going out on the 12 o'clock ride?"

Tom pulled himself together as he realized that Alex had asked him the same question twice.

"N-No," Tom stuttered. "I'm going home. Can you say goodbye to the others for me?"

"Sure," said Alex, puzzled at Tom's strange behavior. It was very unlike him to spend any time away from Sandy Lane.

Thoughtfully, Tom wandered over to his bike. He wanted the afternoon to think about how he could put his plan into action. He also couldn't bear the thought of being around Nick and having to lie to him at the same time. It would be better once he had started the training. Once Chancey had started to improve, it would all seem worth it.

Back at home, Tom slid into the sitting room clutching a pad of note paper. He felt like a criminal.

"Come on, get a grip," he muttered to himself, thinking aloud. "Nick brings the other horses in from the fields at seven thirty, which means we'll have to start at six to be finished in time."

He wrote it all down, chewing the end of his pencil as he figured out his plan. That meant he would have to be up at the stables at five thirty. Tom groaned to himself. It was a very early start. And how long would he have to do it for? Should he make up a training program? Tom churned these thoughts over in his mind for the rest of the day.

* * * * * * * * * * * * * * *

Tom's alarm went off at five fifteen the next morning. Fumbling under his pillow, he switched it off and sat bolt upright. He rubbed his eyes. It was already light outside. Pulling on his jeans, he stole down the stairs and out of the sleepy house. Quickly, he unchained his bike from the drainpipe. His heart was beating fast and there was a knot in his stomach. There would be such trouble if he was caught.

Nothing stirred, nothing rustled, as Tom cycled along. The stables were silent as Tom reached the stables... unnervingly still and quiet as he crept to Chancey's stall.

"Sshh," said Tom, stifling Chancey's whinny with a sugar lump as he hurriedly tacked him up. Tom was sure that Nick would hear the clatter of Chancey's shoes on the gravel as he led him out of his stall and through the gate at the back. Nervously, Tom looked up at the bedroom windows of the house. No one seemed to be up yet. The curtains were tightly drawn and Tom breathed a sigh of relief. Everyone must still be fast asleep. It was only when Tom was in the last of the fields behind the stables that he felt safe... safe away from prying eyes. Tom sprang into the saddle and gathered up the reins.

"Come on Chancey. We've only got an hour and there's a lot to fit in."

Chancey responded promptly to the light squeeze from Tom's calves and went forward into a trot. Automatically, Tom turned him in the direction of Larkfield Copse. They were headed for the beach. Gently, Chancey cantered along, over the fields, through the trees and soon they were on the open stretches beyond. Tom started to relax. This was fun.

As they reached the top of the cliffs, Tom could just make out the distant shape of a ship on the bleak horizon. The tide was out and the beach was deserted at this time of the morning. The wind was whipping up the waves, billowing the water into clouds of spray. Gently, Tom leaned back, putting his hand on Chancey's rump to steady himself as they picked their way down the path from the cliff.

Then they were down on the beach and suddenly they were galloping as though nothing else mattered... along the sand, through the waves and past the caves that he and Alex had discovered only last summer. It was glorious. Tom found it hard to pull Chancey up when there was nothing to stop them from going on and on forever.

"Whoa boy, calm down," said Tom, clapping his hand to Chancey's neck and slowly pulling him up. Chancey snatched at the bit.

"That was just to warm you up," Tom laughed. "We'll have to do some real exercise now – serpentines. Ready?"

Chancey was jumpy as Tom tried to get him to make the 's' shape in the sand. But soon they had perfected the movement, bending from right to left, leaving a trail in the sand like a snake. Tom was miles away, when suddenly he realized the time.

"Oh help!" he cried, looking at his watch. "We'll have to hurry back. We'll ride in the outdoor arena tomorrow," he told Chancey. "It's all well and good going fast, but we'll have to do some flat work and practice some jumping too."

Quietly, they wound their way back to Sandy Lane

and stealthily crept into the stables. It was already twenty after seven. Luckily no one was around this time, still they would have to be more careful about timing in the future. Quickly, Tom put Chancey away in his stall.

"You'll have to wait for your food, Chancey – well, until Nick comes around with the morning feedings anyway."

"You're here early, Tom," a voice boomed out from behind him. Tom nearly jumped out of his skin. "Couldn't keep yourself away from Chancey, eh?" It was Nick.

"Er-I didn't have a very good night's sleep, so I got up and thought I might as well head down here," Tom stuttered. Nick shook his head and smiled. He didn't seem to have noticed anything out of the ordinary. Tom breathed a sigh of relief that he hadn't been discovered. He was sure that his guilt must have been written all over his face.

"Well, you could get going with the feedings anyway," Nick suggested. "By the way, I put up the poster about the local show yesterday. Everyone's very excited about it. It's only three weeks away. Good practice for Benbridge. You could ride Napoleon if you like. No one dared sign up for him. I think they're all scared of you." Nick laughed.

Tom felt a sudden pang of guilt. Napoleon had always been his favorite horse at the stables. Everyone said they looked great together. But since Chancey had arrived... well, Tom couldn't feel the same about any other horse.

"Thanks Nick, I'll go and check it out," said Tom. He didn't dare ask if he could ride Chancey at the local show – he couldn't bear to hear Nick's refusal.

Nick looked puzzled. Normally Tom would have been rushing to sign up by Napoleon.

"I'm sorry, Tom. I don't think I'm going to have a minute to spare to spend with you and Chancey today. It'll have to be tomorrow," he said.

"Oh, don't worry," said Tom. He turned away rather too quickly, hoping that Nick hadn't noticed him reddening. Tom hated going behind Nick's back. He hoped he would be able to live with his conscience over the next few weeks.

7

A NARROW ESCAPE

As the date of the local show drew nearer, Tom proved to be right about Nick -- there simply weren't enough hours in the day for him to take lessons, train Storm Cloud *and* help out with Chancey too. So Tom continued his secret outings, not just to the beach, but in the outdoor arena as well. It was more risky there, as anyone coming early to Sandy Lane would be sure to see them, but Chancey had to get used to an enclosed area. Tom told himself it was worth taking the risk.

Leading Chancey out of his stall that morning, Tom was careful to avoid taking the drive down to the outdoor arena. Although it was the quickest way there, they would be sure to be heard from the house. Tom felt guilty as he rode the long way around through the fields but he told himself it had to be done. His heart started to beat faster. It was only when they had reached the outdoor arena that he started to calm down.

Quickly, he climbed into the saddle and started to limber up. After a quarter of an hour of basic exercise, Chancey was clearly bored.

"Come on," Tom cried impatiently as he tried to drive Chancey into the corners. Chancey wouldn't respond.

"OK. I know you've had enough of that," Tom said. "We'll try some jumping." He dismounted and tethered Chancey to the fence.

"Now, what height had we gotten to?" he asked the horse. "Here?"

Tom raised the post and rails by two feet. Chancey snorted.

"Ah, so you want it higher do you? OK then." Tom grinned as he moved on to the next fence.

It took him a while to raise the jumps, and he would only have to knock them down again once they had finished. It was a nuisance, but better that than risk getting caught. Nick had finished off with a class of beginners yesterday, and there was no way they would have been jumping three and a half feet. It would look highly suspicious if Tom left the jumps as they were.

"Come on boy," he said.

Chancey danced on the spot as Tom showed him the course he had prepared for them.

"Come on, let's go, or it'll be back to lessons for you and I know that you don't want that."

Chancey shook his head and neighed impatiently as he waited for the signal to start. Slowly, Tom nudged him on with his heels and they approached the first. Carefully, they eased their way around the course, clearing each of the jumps in easy succession.

"One more time, Chancey," Tom whispered, turning

the horse back to the start without stopping for a break.

Flying over the post and rails, Chancey went on to soar over the parallel bars. Landing lightly, Tom spun him on the spot for the triple on the far side of the arena. Chancey didn't hesitate as Tom drove him forward. He jumped fluently, his tail swishing as he touched down after the first and went on to clear the next two jumps.

It never failed to amaze Tom how high Chancey could go. Sometimes he thought that he was asking too much of his horse. But Chancey never refused. He was a gutsy creature.

After what seemed like no more than half an hour of jumping, Tom looked at his watch.

"It's already ten after seven," he groaned. "We'll have to stop or we might find we have company."

Dismounting in the drive, Tom led Chancey to his stall and untacked him. Then he hurried back to the arena to knock down the fences. Hurtling around the course, he kicked down the poles as he went. Opening the gate, Tom let himself out as the alarm on his watch started to beep. He had taken to setting it at seven fifteen – the final warning.

"Just in time," Tom said to himself, striding into the stables.

"Morning Tom," Nick called from Hector's stall.

"Morning Nick," Tom replied breezily as he strolled over to Chancey's stall. He wondered how long Nick had been there. A moment longer and they would have been caught red-handed.

"I've got a free hour at nine. We could do some work with Chancey then if you like," said Nick.

"Great," said Tom, trying to muster up some energy.

He wished he hadn't pushed Chancey so hard and hoped he wouldn't be too tired.

"Hi Tom," Jess called cheerfully from across the stables. "Do you think you might find time to help me with the feedings?"

"OK," Tom laughed. Jess wasn't one for hanging around. Together they set to work and by a quarter to ten they had mucked out five stalls, filled eight hay feeders and groomed the horses that were going to be used that morning. They reckoned they had done more than their fair share of work.

"Do you want to go and get Chancey ready?" Nick called.

"Sure," Tom answered, hurrying off.

Chancey looked puzzled when Tom started to tack him up again.

"You're not to give the game away, Chancey," Tom whispered in his horse's ear as he led him down to the arena. Chancey nickered softly.

"All right, Tom. Let's see what you can do," said Nick, opening the gate to the outdoor arena. "That's funny," he called. "I could have sworn the jumps were all standing yesterday. Someone's been messing around in here."

Tom felt embarrassed as Nick went around the course putting the jumps back up.

"OK, are you ready? Take him over the cross poles a couple of times to warm him up and then try this combination, Tom," said Nick. "You shouldn't find it difficult."

It was all the encouragement that Tom needed. With a little nudge of his heels, he urged Chancey on. Chancey cantered forward with long, easy strides, holding his head high, as he cleared the poles. Nick was mesmerized as he watched them moving gracefully around the ring.

"I can't believe how well you're both going together," Nick called from the center of the ring. "It's a pleasure to watch. Each time that I've seen you both, there seems to be an overnight improvement. It's almost as though Chancey goes away after one of our sessions, thinks it all through and puts it into practice the next time around," Nick beamed.

"Yes, yes, I suppose you're right," Tom spluttered.

"Well, he's certainly perfected jumping that double anyway," Nick answered.

So Nick had started to notice a difference. Tom reddened and turned away. They had been practicing the double in secret for almost a week now. And it certainly hadn't been an overnight improvement for Tom. What would Nick say if he ever found out it wasn't just his training that was responsible?

Tom felt nervous. Nick wasn't the only one who had noticed some changes. His mother had been complaining that Tom was spending too much time down at Sandy Lane. Tom was scared that if he wasn't careful, she might say something to Nick and Sarah. He couldn't have that happening. And he didn't dare admit to his mother that the owners of Sandy Lane didn't even know he was down there so early in the mornings. He would be caught without a doubt. There was no alternative, he would have to limit the amount of time he was spending with Chancey.

As Tom led Chancey back to the stables, he thought how complicated it was all getting. He didn't know how much longer he could go on with it all. Training

Chancey and trying to keep it a secret was completely exhausting him. Nevertheless, Chancey was getting better. Tom tried to tell himself it would be worth it in the end. Little did he know how close that end would be... that his plans were soon to be brought to an abrupt halt.

8

THE WARNING

Over a week had passed and Chancey was acting up yet again. When Tom asked him to canter, he trotted faster. When Tom wanted him to halt, he kept on walking. It was as though he was being contrary on purpose, trying to tell Tom that he was bored and would rather be doing something he enjoyed more. He would never make a dressage horse, Tom knew that. So Tom decided to give up the flat work and jump him instead. And he was jumping beautifully.

"I'm not going to give in to you every time you misbehave, Chancey. Only this once. I like jumping as much as you do, but you've got to learn the ground rules too."

Tom raised the triple. Was it asking too much? Taking a deep breath, he faced Chancey at the spread.

It was a difficult combination, with only one horse stride between each of the jumps, but Chancey didn't hesitate as he approached the first. Sitting back on his hocks, he rocked backward and released himself through the air like a coil. Springing over the jumps, he cleared them one by one with at least a foot to spare. Tom couldn't remember ever feeling so exhilarated.

"Wait until the next time Nick trains us," he whispered, slapping Chancey's neck so hard that it echoed like thunder around the arena. "He'll be so pleased." And then Tom stopped and sighed. How long would it be before Nick could train them again? Certainly it wouldn't be that day. Nick had already told Tom that he was going to be busy giving lessons.

Tom knew that he shouldn't grumble. In the summer months there were so many vacationers around... business was booming. It was exactly what Nick and Sarah needed and at least it made Tom feel less guilty that Chancey wasn't bringing in any money.

Tom was miles away when he felt conscious that they weren't alone. Someone was watching them. A solitary figure stood leaning against the fence. Tom's heart skipped a beat. He knew immediately who it was. They had been caught. What could he say? Tentatively, Tom walked Chancey over to the gate and took a deep breath.

"Hello Tom," said Nick. There was a strained silence between them.

"How long has this been going on then?" he continued calmly. There was no inflection in Nick's voice for Tom to decide how to play things.

That was Nick all over, no words of reproach, just a composed question. It would have been easier if there had been angry words. Tom could have handled that. But Nick's restraint made it even worse. Tom tried to summon up courage.

"Nearly three weeks now. I didn't want to go behind your back, Nick. I had to." Tom swallowed hard. "We just weren't going to be ready for Benbridge otherwise. Chancey's going so well. Wait until you see him. You can't be angry then," he said nervously.

"There will be no seeing him," replied Nick in a quiet rage. "What do you think you're doing? I can't have you setting this kind of example to the others. You could have been hurt. Who would get the blame then?" Tom had never seen Nick this angry before.

"I was only trying to help. I didn't mean any harm," Tom gasped, tears welling in his eyes. He rubbed them away with his sleeve, annoyed that he hadn't been able to stop himself.

"Please look at him, Nick. He's awesome. I only wanted to get him started. We just weren't getting anywhere. I know that you've been busy but... but..."

There was an uncomfortable pause. Nick knew it was true. He had been too tied up with other things to help Tom and Chancey and he had said that he would. He did feel a little guilty, but a promise was a promise. Tom had overstepped the mark this time. Nick looked long and hard. Should he let them show him what they could do?

"I shouldn't, Tom. But I'll give you one last chance," he said quickly, softening a little. "Eleven o'clock this morning. I'll see you after the class of little ones. We'll take it from there." He turned on his heels.

Tom was left clutching Chancey's reins, his riding hat sliding down over his eyes. Trudging off to Chancey's stall, there was a faint glimmer of hope.

"We'll show them. We'll show them all." Tom

gritted his teeth. He untacked Chancey and put some food in the corner. When Chancey had finished eating, Tom began to groom him, starting with the legs and working up.

It didn't take long before the others knew what had happened. News spread quickly at Sandy Lane. They all felt sorry for Tom, but at the same time couldn't quite believe what he had done. None of them would have been as daring themselves.

"I'd never have guessed," said Jess, turning her back to Rosie as she gave a little girl a leg-up onto Blackjack.

"Poor Tom," said Rosie.

"I half suspected something was up," said Alex. "He's been really strange... so secretive."

The others all nodded in agreement.

"We normally do so much together," Alex went on in a hurt voice. "And we just haven't lately."

"I wonder what Chancey will be like this time," said Jess. "Tom must be pretty confident if he's prepared to show Nick."

Tom did feel confident. Only that morning, Chancey had jumped the triple with ease. Nick would be so impressed, he simply couldn't be angry. He would let Tom enter the local show on Chancey; they would be able to use Chancey for lessons; things would be all right.

Tom busied himself around the stables, desperately trying to keep out of Nick's way until the allotted time. At ten to eleven, he went to get ready. Chancey was on his toes as Tom tacked him up.

"Come on, boy. Calm down," Tom soothed.

"Where do you want to try him, Tom?" Nick asked, peering over the door.

"Oh, anywhere really," said Tom.

"We'll try him in the ring then," Nick said.

Tom led Chancey out of his stall and sprang confidently into the saddle. As they headed down the drive, Chancey pirouetted, snorting as Tom gathered up the reins.

As Nick opened the gate, they entered the outdoor arena. Tom felt uneasy. Nick frowned. There was a sense of foreboding in the air. Suddenly Tom didn't feel quite so confident.

Tom didn't even have a chance to show Nick what they could do. As the engine of a car roared in the distance, Chancey's ears flashed back and he started bucking like a maniac. Tom hadn't seen it coming. Before he knew it, he was flung to the ground and Chancey was tearing toward the gate. He looked as though he was going to cannon straight into it. But without hesitating, he launched himself over it and charged down the road like a rocket.

"Did you see that?" Alex cried excitedly. "Never mind him being crazy. That was a five-barred gate he cleared and with miles to spare. I can't believe it."

Tom had landed heavily but the sand in the arena had acted as a cushion. He sat rooted to the spot. His head was in his hands, his face was ashen, white with shock. Panic rose in his throat.

"What if he falls? He'll break his knees and then he'll be ruined. He'll have to be put down, and it will be all my fault. We've got to catch him," he said, struggling to his feet.

"We'll take the truck, Tom," Nick said angrily. "I knew something like this would happen. He'll be miles away by now. This was the very reason I didn't want you riding him."

"He's been going so well for me though," said Tom. "I don't know what's got into him. Maybe the noise of the cars on the road startled him."

"Maybe he just wasn't ready to be handled by a novice."

Nick's heated words stung Tom to the core as he realized the enormity of what had happened.

"Come on. Let's go," said Nick. "We have to try and catch him. If he's actually on the road, who knows what could happen. If he causes an accident, Sandy Lane would be liable."

"Grab a halter, Tom. I'll go and tell Sarah," he said, hurrying off toward the house.

Moments later he reappeared. Climbing into the truck, they rattled off down the drive and out of the stables.

"Keep your eyes peeled, Tom," said Nick. "I'll drive slowly past these trees and you look in."

Tom couldn't see any movement in the thicket of pines. Chancey was nowhere to be seen. Nick drove on and on... past miles and miles of hedgerow, but although there were plenty of horses in the surrounding fields, Chancey was not among them. Tom's heart missed a beat as he saw a chestnut horse, but his hopes sank as the horse's white face turned to look at him.

Two hours of solid driving, down every road and through every field that Nick could think of, and still they hadn't found him. Tom was almost in despair.

"Where can he be? We've tried practically everywhere," he wailed, his voice rising into hysteria.

"Calm down, Tom. He'll have to stop somewhere. Let's go back to the stables and see if there's any news, do some phoning around. Someone may have called the police by now," Nick said despondently.

As they rounded the corner to Sandy Lane, Rosie came rushing out to meet them.

"It's all right, Chancey's been found. He's safe. Alex managed to catch him. He was grazing in the fields behind the stables. He must have found his own way home."

Tom rushed forward to Chancey's stall to see for himself. Sure enough, there was Chancey, peacefully munching from a hay feeder as if nothing had happened. He looked up as Tom approached and whinnied softly. His eyes were bright and clear as he pushed his head forward and his lips nuzzled Tom for a tidbit.

"Not today, Chancey. You're not having a reward today," Tom said furiously. "You've done it this time." The others crowded anxiously around Tom.

"Tom, Tom, he was amazing," said Alex breathlessly, his eyes glinting with excitement. "I can't believe how he cleared that gate. He was born to jump. You were right, he has got it in him."

A hush fell over the group as Nick approached. No one dared breathe as they waited to hear what he had to say.

"Well Tom," said Nick. "There's nothing more to say. I had forbidden you to ride him before and I am forbidding you again. He's dangerous. If you go against my word this time, then you'll not only be forbidden to ride Chancey, you'll be out of Sandy Lane... for good."

9

THE LOCAL SHOW

Tom was at loose ends in the days following the warning. It was so unfair. Chancey had been going so well for him in secret. It must have been the noise of the car that had startled him. What bad luck for it to happen in front of Nick. And now, how could Tom ever prove that Chancey wasn't the crazed animal everyone thought he was, if he wasn't even allowed to ride him? In the end, it was Alex who came up with the solution... the perfect solution.

They were sitting in the dark in the tack room. It was late in the day and dusk had just started to set in. Nick was out with a class and the others had all gone home, leaving only Tom and Alex to clean the tack. Tom was polishing Chancey's saddle so hard that he could almost see his reflection in it.

"Look I'm sorry Alex," said Tom. "I know I should have told you what I was up to. It's just that I felt bad enough having to go behind Nick's back. I didn't want you to have to do it as well."

"I could have helped you though," said Alex in a hurt voice. "We could have done things together. I could have covered for you until you were one hundred percent ready to show Chancey to Nick."

"That's the trouble," said Tom gloomily. "I thought we were one hundred percent ready. I've been training him for weeks now and he's been getting better and better. It's the first trouble I've been into... typical that it had to be then of all times." Tom sighed. "What can I do?"

"There's only one thing to do Tom," said Alex. "You've got to prove to Nick that all your training was worth it, that he is the horse you know he is."

"How am I going to be able to do that now?" asked Tom.

"Well." Alex took a deep breath. "Ride him at the local show."

"That's impossible," Tom spluttered. "I've been forbidden to go near him. You heard what Nick said – I'd be out of Sandy Lane."

"Yes, but if Chancey matters that much, and you know you're right... you're down to ride Napoleon at the moment aren't you?"

"Yes," said Tom.

"So why not switch mounts and ride Chancey instead? By the time Nick realizes what's happened, it'll be too late for him to stop you. And when you've won, you'll have proved your point and he won't be angry any more."

"What if he is still angry?" said Tom. "And suppose Chancey and I can't do it? What if he acts up again?

It's risking everything."

"It's all you can do though. It's a gamble I know. But it's a gamble you have to take. I'll help you," Alex continued encouragingly. "I'm not riding in the open jumping which will give me the perfect opportunity to go and switch Napoleon's name for Chancey's at the show secretary's tent."

"Would you do that for me?" asked Tom.

"Yes, but we must keep it a secret. If anyone finds out, our plan will be ruined."

"OK," said Tom.

Tom was hesitant at first. But as the days passed, he started to feel more and more sure that Alex was right, that it was the only way.

* * * * * * * * * * * * * * *

The day of the local show dawned cool and clear. The stables seethed with excitement as the horses were washed, groomed and braided. Tom groomed Chancey in secret and doubled back to get him once everyone had left Sandy Lane. The show was only two miles away, so it didn't take Tom long to ride him over there.

There was no going back now. The open jumping class had started an hour ago and there were only ten minutes until Tom was due in the ring. Nervously, he paced up and down in the woods. No doubt the others would be running around looking for him, panicking as Napoleon stood tied to the horse van, unattended and riderless. Tom felt a stab of guilt. Napoleon was a good horse and loved these shows, but Tom told himself he had to do it, for Chancey's sake.

Meanwhile, all he could do was wait. The hubbub of the crowd filled the showground and the smell of hot dogs hung in the air. Tom felt sick to the bottom of his stomach as he thought of what lay ahead of him. He had gone over the course again and again in his mind. It was fairly straightforward, Chancey should be able to walk it. But as they hadn't had time to practice since Nick's warning, Tom kept having little doubts. What if he was the one to mess up and let them down?

Tom's shoulders felt stiff and wooden, his hands clammy, as he mounted and started to loosen Chancey up in the woods away from the showground. He mustn't let Chancey sense he was nervous. He had to stay calm and collected if they were to stand a chance. Tom buttoned up his jacket and secured his chin strap. And then he heard his name being called.

"Number sixty-five... Tom Buchanan on Horton Chancellor," the voice called over the loudspeaker.

On the other side of the ring, Nick raised his head in astonishment at the announcement.

Tom cantered over to the ring and acknowledged the judges. He rode a circle, waiting for the bell.

R-r-ring. Tom was off. Nothing else was important. Nobody else mattered. His mind was focused on one thing, and one thing only – to jump clear. Chancey looked magnificent as he headed for the first jump in a collected canter. His nostrils flared and his eyes flashed amber as he gathered his pace.

"Go on, Tom, you can do it," Alex muttered as Tom

pushed Chancey forward.

Tom couldn't hear him though. His mind was set on the course ahead. Concentration flickered across his face as the crowd became a blur of faces for him.

They were over the first and on to the gate. Tom felt Chancey speed up and tried to steady him. Soaring over the gate, they approached the stile. They were clear. Turning back on themselves, they raced up the middle to jump the triple.

"One, two, three," Alex muttered as Chancey bounded over the fences. One more turn to come, then the parallel bars and finally the huge wall. Chancey leapt over the parallel bars nimbly and went on to fly over the wall, clearing it with ease. And then they were cantering through the finish to the sound of applause, as the voice announced the result.

"Tom Buchanan on Horton Chancellor, jumping clear with no time faults and into the jump-off."

Tom grinned to himself. They were through to the next round.

"Way to go boy. You were awesome." He patted Chancey proudly as the admiring spectators looked on at him. And then he saw Nick.

Tom looked at him pleadingly. Nick's eyes flashed angrily.

"What do you think you're doing, Tom?" he said. "Finish the round and see me afterward."

Tom felt sick again. They must win.

There were four competitors through to the jump-off, and Tom was third in the ring. Not a bad place, he thought to himself. He watched the other competitors from behind the rails, carefully weighing up the opposition. The first competitor had a bad round and sent everything crashing to the floor. The second competitor, a girl in immaculate cream britches and navy riding jacket, set a better standard. She looked incredibly professional and for a moment Tom doubted that he should really be competing against her. She jumped clear.

Then it was Tom's turn. He cantered the obligatory circle, looked determinedly straight ahead and approached the first.

There was a loud bang as Chancey rapped the top of the rails. Tom's heart sank. He looked under his arm. But it was all right, the pole was still hanging there – how, he didn't know but it was still there. The near miss at the first fence had startled Chancey and he went on to clear the gate by miles, careful to pick his feet up as they flew over it. Collecting his stride, Tom faced Chancey at the stile, leaning forward to take his weight off his back. Tucking his legs up under him, Chancey sailed neatly over the jump.

Almost turning on the spot, Tom swung him around and they raced up the middle for the triple. Chancey cleared the three jumps with ease. Tom knew his horse, knew how far he could push him and with another sharp turn, Chancey sprang gracefully over the parallel bars and again there was only the wall. The crowd held their breath as horse and rider rose to the challenge. They were over it!

Everyone cheered madly as the voice announced that Tom Buchanan and Horton Chancellor had taken the lead with a time of three minutes and sixteen seconds.

"What a speed. No one will be able to beat that," Alex said excitedly to a stranger standing next to him.

And sure enough, the last rider wasn't able to beat Tom's time and it seemed only moments later that Tom was galloping around the ring, a blue ribbon attached to Chancey's bridle.

Nick was the first to meet him as he came out of the ring. Tom looked shamefaced. Nick smiled. He had hardly been able to contain himself during the jump-off. And there was something else too. Tom reminded Nick of how he had been as a boy. If he was totally honest with himself, he knew that he would have done exactly the same thing.

"Way to go, Tom. You were both magnificent," he grinned.

Tom felt jubilant. It was to be a good day for all of them. Alex went on to win a second in the novice jumping, Kate a third in the show class, Jess a second in the pole race and Rosie a first in the potato race.

"OK, Tom. You've proved your point," Nick said on the way home. "We're going to have to step up the Benbridge campaign now. After all, you'll be representing Sandy Lane there. And don't think I don't know who put you up to this." He turned and grinned at Alex.

Tom smiled wearily. It had been an exhausting day, both mentally and physically. All the worry about how Nick would react had taken its toll and the early morning outings had finally caught up with him.

"Everyone was talking about you, Tom," said Kate. "Everybody wanted to know who Chancey was. I wouldn't be surprised if you had quite a few offers for him after that amazing performance."

Kate was trying to be friendly, but her words rang alarm bells in Tom's head. Of course people would be interested in Chancey – he was wonderful. But Chancey wasn't his. Tom's heart felt heavy at the thought. He sighed. He couldn't be anything but a loser, for Benbridge meant the end of the summer, the return of Georgina and the loss of the horse to whom he had become so deeply attached.

10

AN UNWANTED VISITOR

Life at Sandy Lane was kind of an anticlimax after the drama of the show. The only stir of excitement was caused by the arrival of entry forms for Benbridge. Tom was well aware that he would face much stiffer competition there than at the local show. Chancey would have to be at his very best if they were to have any hope of winning.

And there was something that was preying on Tom's mind – something he had been putting off doing. Four days had already passed since the local show, if he didn't say something soon, he never would.

"Nick, I was wondering if you would like to use Chancey in lessons now," Tom said hesitantly.

"That's a very generous offer, Tom," Nick said thoughtfully.

Tom's face dropped. Although he knew it was about time Chancey paid his way at Sandy Lane, Tom

69

couldn't bear the thought of anyone else riding him.

"But I think it would be better if you alone rode him now that he's grown used to you," Nick continued, "until Benbridge anyway. Besides, we don't really need him. You could say we're overloaded with horses now that Feather's back in action and Storm Cloud wasn't such a disaster buy."

Tom breathed a sigh of relief and strolled over to the hay bales by the old barn to join Alex and Jess. He took out the packed lunch that his mother now allowed him to take to Sandy Lane. It had been a long battle, until finally she had agreed that there was no point in him coming all the way home at lunch time only to wolf down his food and hurry back again. Tom was also quick to point out that the other children had their lunches at Sandy Lane. Tom knew that his mother wouldn't want to seem less reasonable than other mothers.

Tom spread out the Benbridge entry form in front of him and munched happily on his sandwiches.

"Which classes are you going to enter, Tom?" asked Kate, as she joined him on the bales.

"Oh, only the open jumping. Chancey would hate the show classes. He'd never manage to stand still for long enough," Tom laughed.

"Well, I've entered absolutely everything," said Kate. "I don't care which classes I win, just as long as Minstrel's plastered with ribbons – though we've probably got the best chance in the hunters," she said, blinking in the brilliant sunshine. "It's so bright out here. I can hardly see this entry form. Where do you put your name?"

"Here, silly," said Rosie, who had wandered across

the stable grounds and was looking over Kate's shoulder. They were all together now, all of the Sandy Lane regulars. Nick had selected Tom, Kate and Alex to ride at Benbridge after their successes at the local show but both Rosie and Jess intended to go as well to support their friends.

"Well, I'm still pretty excited about my first in the potato race," said Rosie smiling. "Although I'd rather it had been in something a little more graceful. My brothers howled with laughter when I told them."

Tom looked at his watch. Two thirty. He had work to do with Chancey. Sarah was taking the others down to the beach for a ride.

As much as Tom loved the beach, Nick had said that he would train them for an hour in the ring. And with Benbridge less than two weeks away, it was an offer he couldn't refuse. He packed away what was left of his lunch and headed, sandwich in mouth, to Chancey's stall.

Chancey's head appeared over the door as Tom held out the carrot that his mother had packed. He smiled to himself. Perhaps she was starting to feel some affection for his four-legged friend. Chancey stretched out his neck and sniffed apprehensively at the offering.

"It's not going to bite, silly," Tom laughed.

Once Chancey was sure that it was edible, his silky lips mumbled over Tom's flat hand, and in an instant the carrot disappeared. It made Tom laugh to see Chancey so careful with his food yet so bold when he jumped. Slipping into the stall, Tom tacked him up and led him out into the stables. The others were making a racket getting their mounts ready for their beach ride. Tom had to muster up all his willpower to stop himself from turning around and going too. It would be wonderful on the beach at this time of day.

"See you later, Tom," Sarah called. "Tell Nick we'll be back by four. Certainly no later anyway as it's high tide at four."

"OK, I'll tell him," Tom answered.

At low tide, the wide expanse of beach at Sandy Bay was clear, but when the tide came in, the sand was flooded. If you weren't careful, you could find yourself cut off from land. Nick was careful to post a monthly copy of tide times on the tack room door and insisted that everyone check it before planning a ride to the beach. It was one of the first things that Tom had learned about when he had started at Sandy Lane.

"Right, Tom," said Nick, stepping out of the tack room. "Let's go. I've set up a course for you in the outdoor arena. See what you make of it. There's one difficult jump. But I think you'll handle it all right."

"OK," said Tom. Forgetting the beach ride in an instant, he headed off to the outdoor arena. Its white fence looked crisp in the bright sunshine, contrasting sharply with the brightly painted jumps. Nick had erected a figure eight for them to practice over. Chancey eyed the course suspiciously. The hard jump proved to be a square oxer.

"Parallel bars – difficult for a horse to judge the stretch and clear," Tom muttered to himself.

"I'll watch you for a while, Tom," said Nick, jumping up onto the fence. "Then I've got to go and take a private group for a ride."

Tom trotted Chancey around the arena and pushed him on into an easy canter.

"Take him around once more, Tom," said Nick. "It'll

make him more balanced when he starts jumping and it'll settle his rhythm too."

"OK," said Tom and swiftly they cantered once around the ring.

"Ready? You could take him over the course now, Tom," Nick called. "I want you to approach the first two jumps at a trot. It's good training for him."

Tom circled Chancey one more time and then popped him over the post and rails. Trotting him over the stile, he turned him wide at the corner of the arena to give him enough time to see the square oxer. Chancey had been paying attention and, with a little encouragement from Tom, stepped up his pace to leap over the jump, clearing it easily. Collectedly, Tom rode across the arena on a diagonal for the double.

"Be careful that you don't anticipate the jump and lean forward too early, Tom," Nick's voice boomed from the side of the arena. "Let Chancey find his natural takeoff point, otherwise you'll unbalance him and he'll try to put in an extra stride. Then you'll be the one who's unbalanced," he said laughing. "Otherwise, pretty good. It's as though he's a different horse."

"He's always like this with me now, Nick," Tom shouted back. "I think he has gotten used to me. He trusts me."

"I think you're right. Try him again," said Nick. "Then I really will have to go and get ready for this lesson."

Tom and Chancey soared around the course, unaware that Nick had crept away, leaving them to it. Jump after jump was cleared in swift succession until eventually Tom pulled Chancey to a halt. Leaping nimbly to the ground, he tethered him to the fence.

"That was just for practice," he said mischievously, as he went around the course raising the jumps. "Now this should wake you up."

Tom never had any sense of time when he jumped Chancey. Now, he was so involved with his riding, that he didn't notice the girl watching them from the shade of the cedar tree. Sulkily, she stared out at them, screwing up her sallow face as she took it all in.

All that could be heard was the sound of Chancey's hooves pounding against the ground as Tom and Chancey sailed over the jumps. Soon the others would be returning from their ride, and the stables would be buzzing with activity while everyone began clearing up the grounds for the evening. Little did Tom know of what lay ahead of him. Happily, he jumped off Chancey to raise the jumps again, not satisfied until he had stretched them both to the limit.

"Right. That's it for now, boy," he said tiredly, as they knocked down a jump in the last round. "You're exhausted." Chancey's sides were puffing in and out like bellows. "You've had enough for one day. I don't want to push you too far."

Idly, he made his way to the gate and slid off the horse as the girl stepped out from the shadow of the tree. Tom was startled. The sun shone in his eyes as he returned the stony gaze of the girl who stood opposite him.

"Georgina," he gasped. "What are you doing back?"

11

FROM BAD TO WORSE

Tom couldn't believe his eyes. His cousin Georgina was standing right in front of him. Her cold blue eyes stared out at him from her pallid face. What was she doing here? She wasn't due back for another three weeks. Tom blinked, anxiously.

"I've come back early so I can ride Horton Chancellor at the Benbridge show," Georgina said quickly.

Tom's heart skipped a beat as he stared at the defiant face of his cousin. His worst nightmare was coming true. He felt a lump rising in his throat, almost choking him.

"Then are you taking him home today?" Tom asked, stumbling over the words.

"Oh no," Georgina said haughtily. "Change of plan. Daddy's tired of having him at home, says it's too much work for him. I'm supposed to arrange with the owners of Sandy Lane to keep him on here at half-board or something. Do you know them?"

"Of course I do," Tom said. Thoughts raced through his mind. Benbridge... keeping him at Sandy Lane... half-board. Tom dismounted and, taking the reins in his right hand, led Chancey off to his stall.

"You'd better come with me," he said. "I'll take you to meet Nick. Do you want to take Chancey to his stall?"

"No, that's all right, you can do it," said Georgina breezily. "There'll be plenty of time for me to spend with him."

"OK, fine. Here's Nick now," he said as Nick strode toward them.

"What's going on?" Nick asked, as Tom hurriedly tried to explain the situation, holding on to a very jumpy Chancey.

"This is my cousin, Georgina," said Tom, "the owner of Horton Chancellor. She would like to talk to you about the possibility of boarding him with you."

"Oh, I see," said Nick thoughtfully. "Well, you'd better come and discuss things at the house with my wife Sarah, then." He tried to catch Tom's eye, but Tom had already turned away.

"So this is it then, boy," said Tom when he was alone with Chancey. "Your owner has come back to claim you, although earlier than expected."

Tom felt numb. He didn't know what he had thought would happen when Georgina returned. He had put it to the back of his mind for so long, half-hoping that she would never come back, half-hoping that she would forget about the horse altogether. Unrealistic dreams. He sighed.

"What's going on, Tom?" asked Rosie, leaning over the stall door and looking into Chancey's box.

"It's my cousin, Georgina," Tom said sadly. "She's back."

"Oh," said Rosie. "That's a little early isn't it?" The words tumbled from her mouth before she had a chance to stop them.

"Yes it is," said Tom, turning away. Rosie could have kicked herself for being so thoughtless. She could see the hurt in Tom's eyes and wished she knew what to say to make him feel better.

"Er, I'm going home," she mumbled feebly. "What are you going to do now?"

"I don't know," said Tom. "Hang around here I suppose. I want to wait and see what Nick has to say."

"Oh," she said awkwardly. "Well, I'll see you tomorrow then."

"Yes, see you tomorrow," Tom said quietly as Rosie scuttled away.

Tom didn't have to wait long. He was the first person that Nick wanted to see before he made any decisions. He was well aware how attached Tom had become to the horse.

"Are you OK, Tom? I suppose you knew that she would be back at some point. Still, it doesn't make it any less of a shock, does it? I could say that there isn't any room for her to stable him here if it would make it easier for you."

"No, don't do that Nick," said Tom quickly. "That would make it so much worse. At least if he's here I can see him, even if he isn't really mine."

"I suppose you know that they're only asking to keep him on at half-board," said Nick. "That would mean you could at least ride him when Georgina isn't here. Although I've got some bad news. She's insisting that she rides him at Benbridge."

"I know, she was quick to tell me that," Tom said bitterly.

"I did try telling her about all the work you'd put in and about the rights and wrongs of it, but she wasn't interested," said Nick. "Look Tom, if it's any consolation, I'm entered on Feather for the open jumping at Benbridge. And I would be a lot happier if you rode her in my place. You know I don't like competitions much."

"But..."

"No buts," said Nick. "You would be representing Sandy Lane." Tom smiled and nodded in hesitant acceptance as he turned for home.

Tom's mother knew immediately that something was wrong when he trudged into the kitchen where she was washing up.

"What is it? What is it, darling? You look as though you've seen a ghost," she said.

"You could say that," said Tom. "It's Georgina, you see. She's... she's back." He could hardly get the words out. "She wants to ride Chancey at Benbridge."

"What do you mean?" asked his mother. "She's not due back for another three weeks."

"Sh-she's come back early to ride at Benbridge," he stammered.

Mrs. Buchanan didn't know what to say. She couldn't bear to see the look of disappointment on her son's face. Benbridge was all that he had talked about for weeks. She knew her niece though. If Georgina had her mind set on something, she would never be made to change it.

"Well, perhaps Nick would let you ride one of the other horses," she said halfheartedly, knowing that her solution offered no real consolation.

"He has," said Tom. "But it's not the same."

* * * * * * * * * * * * * * *

When Tom woke the next day, he did so with a heavy heart. The sky was a deep cobalt blue. It was going to be a scorching summer's day. But Tom was in no hurry to get up. He couldn't face the thought of putting on a brave face and going down to Sandy Lane. Tom sighed. There were only ten days until Benbridge now. He owed it to Feather. On the count of ten, he forced himself out of bed.

Tom didn't get to the stables until 10 o'clock and when he did, he was furious to find Chancey still waiting to be groomed.

"What's going on Nick?" asked Tom. "Why isn't Chancey ready?"

"Hmm, I was wondering about that myself. I was under strict instructions from Georgina to leave him. She said that she would be down here to take care of him. Looks as though she might have overslept."

"Might have guessed," said Tom. "I suppose I'd better get it started then."

Tom was just getting the last pieces of straw out of Chancey's tail when Georgina sauntered calmly into the stables.

"Where do you think you've been?" said Tom angrily. "You can't just turn up when you feel like it if you've got a horse to look after."

"Now hang on a minute, Tom," Georgina crowed. "I don't have to answer to you. You're not my mother." Her blue eyes flashed scornfully at him. "Nick, I'm still booked in for the beach ride this morning, aren't I?" she asked, grabbing the brush from Tom as Nick passed by.

"That's right," he replied.

Tom groaned. He was booked to ride Feather on that very ride. Kate was on Jester, Jess had signed up for Minstrel, Rosie was riding Pepper and Alex was on Hector – all on their favorite horses. As it was such a beautiful day, Tom certainly wasn't going to give it up because Georgina would be there. Besides, he needed to make the most of his time with Feather if they were going to be ready for Benbridge.

"Now," said Nick, as everyone gathered around. "For those who are new to Sandy Lane... Georgina, are you listening? I'm only going to say it once."

"Yes Nick," she said sulkily, pulling her blonde hair into a pony tail as her reins trailed by Chancey's side.

Nick started again. "For all of you who don't know, there are strict rules about riding on the beach. First, always keep behind the horse in front of you. And secondly, although it's not applicable this morning, always check the tide sheet on the tack room door when planning a ride to the beach. The tide rolls in very quickly on this part of the coast and you could find yourselves cut off. At the very latest, you must be at the path to the cliffs by the time the water reaches

Gull Rock, which is half an hour before high tide. Sandy Lane won't accept responsibility for anyone disobeying the ground rules. Is that clear?"

"Yes Nick," came back a chorus of voices.

"Right then. Now that's out of the way, let's go."

Turning Whispering Silver to the gate, Nick led the riders out of the stables. In single file, they made their way around the outside of the first field and trotted on to the field of stubble beyond. They chattered excitedly as they made their way to Larkfield Copse. It was a path that Tom knew well. It was the first place he had had a real ride on Chancey... a real ride. He sighed. It seemed so long ago now. Tom cringed as he saw Georgina jab Chancey in the mouth as they entered the woods. He wanted to tell her that she didn't need a riding crop, but knew that it would only be causing trouble for himself. Now she was pulling on the reins and yet driving him on with her heels. No wonder Chancey was confused. Tom had to look away.

A gentle breeze flurried through the trees. Tom looked up, but couldn't see the blue of the sky, hidden as it was by a blanket of leaves.

As they emerged from the shade of the copse, the August sun bore down on their backs. Tom looked behind him at the line of trotting horses as they crossed the old coastal track to the open stretches. It was a lovely sight. Tom could smell the salt in the air as they cantered along the cliff tops.

Tom gazed down at the beach below as Feather sniffed the air. Slowly, the horses picked their way down the cliff path. Once on the sand, Chancey seemed even more edgy and looked as though he might launch himself forward at any moment. Georgina yanked at his head as they trotted along the shoreline.

"Try not to fight with him for his head, Georgina," Nick called out, seeing that she was having trouble. Georgina scowled.

Chancey's neck tightened as Georgina sawed furiously on the reins. He was beginning to foam at the mouth and the hollows of his nostrils were a blood red as he struggled. Tom looked on grimly.

"OK everybody. Let's canter," said Nick. "Remember, it's not a race. Alex, you set off first and we'll follow on."

Alex pushed Hector on into a stiff canter, setting a pace for the others to follow. Soon they were streaming along behind him. Minstrel followed on Hector's toes, then came Kate, Rosie, Georgina and Tom. Nick brought up the rear with Whispering Silver.

Before Tom knew what was happening, he saw Georgina push Chancey on into a gallop. They had overtaken a pretty startled looking Rosie and were wildly out of control as they overtook Kate and Jess and went neck and neck with Hector. Realizing that a race was on, the horses turned into a stampede as they bolted along the beach. Tom tried to pull Feather back gently but he couldn't stop her. His face felt taut as the wind whistled past.

Eventually, Chancey had had enough of racing and seemed to be tiring. He slowed down and soon he was gently cantering... trotting... walking. Tom breathed a sigh of relief. Nick was going to be furious but at least they had managed to stop. The others drew to a halt behind him. Rosie looked as white as a sheet.

"Georgina, did you listen to a word I said?" Nick

asked angrily.

"Yes," she replied insolently. "But I didn't want to go so slowly for all of the ride," she smiled, at what she thought were her new friends.

"As long as you ride at Sandy Lane, you ride under my rules," Nick roared. "Is that clear?"

"Yes Nick," said Georgina, pulling a face as he turned away.

With that, Nick led the riders on the route back to Sandy Lane. He didn't say a word, but it was obvious that he was livid. Tom himself was deep in thought as they rode back. He felt as though there was a black cloud hanging over him. It had really upset him to see Chancey egged on like that. He didn't want to sit by and watch the horse ruined. He would have to keep out of Chancey and Georgina's way, for the time being anyway. He would still go to visit Chancey with a daily tidbit, only he would have to make sure that he wasn't in any classes with them.

There were nine days now to the Benbridge show. Tom wasn't going to be driven away from Sandy Lane because Georgina had come back. He would just spend more time with Feather. She might not have Chancey's strength, she might not have his all-encompassing courage, but she was a talented horse. And Tom was sure that they would go well at Benbridge.

12

BENBRIDGE!

The stables were busier than normal on the morning of the Benbridge show. Everyone was rushing around oiling hooves, searching for grooming tools, braiding manes, putting studs in hooves, and so it went on. By nine o'clock, everyone was ready and the last of the horses were loaded and ready.

In spite of everything, Tom felt excited. Feather was easily the best of Nick and Sarah's horses. And at least Chancey was going to be at Benbridge, even if they wouldn't be sharing the same experience. He also had the added bonus that he didn't have to share the ride to Benbridge with Georgina. Tom smiled to himself.

Nick had thought that it would be too much to have Georgina in the horse van with Tom, so Sarah and the others had been lumbered with her in the Bronco. She had already been complaining that she hadn't expected Chancey to have to share a van. Nick had soon shut her up by telling her that she didn't have to be taken to the show.

Of the Sandy Lane team, Kate had entered Jester in the pony hunter class, Alex had entered Hector for the novice jumping and Tom and Georgina were down for the open jumping. Tom hoped that just because Georgina was arriving with them, people wouldn't think she was Sandy Lane trained. Her aggressive style of riding would do the stables' reputation no good whatsoever.

As they arrived, Tom's eyes widened. He had forgotten what it was like at a big show. It was all so official, so serious. Entries were being announced over a loudspeaker. Officials were running around. There was a stand for the judges. It even *smelled* important. Tom felt a knot in the pit of his stomach.

A steward glanced at their parking permit and waved them on their way. Nick brought the horse van to a halt under the shade of a tree and Tom jumped out of the cab. Heading to the rear of the van, he put down the ramp to let out the horses. Tom was leading out Chancey when the Bronco pulled up next to them and Georgina jumped out.

"Give him here," she cried, grabbing the halter from Tom's hand. Chancey's eyes rolled as she yanked his head to the ring on the side of the horse van.

"I'd be careful with him if I were you, Georgina," said Alex. "You know how jumpy he can get."

"Nonsense. You've got to show them who's boss," Georgina argued.

"Well, let's not spoil such a wonderful day by squabbling anyway," said Kate sensibly. "Come on everyone, we should go and collect our entry numbers.

Tom, you and Georgina had better let them know of your change of horses."

"You're right," said Tom. Wandering over to the secretary's tent, they picked up their numbers and fastened them onto their backs importantly.

"They're huge," said Kate laughing. "It'll cover my whole back."

"That's the general idea," said Georgina.

"I'm going to throttle her if she doesn't shut up," Kate muttered under her breath. "She's such a know-it-all."

Tom smiled to himself. He was used to Georgina. He wasn't going to let her get to him... not today of all days.

"Can someone help me with my hair?" Kate mumbled, her mouth full of bobby pins. "I can't seem to get it all in this hair net. I wish we didn't have to wear them." She scrambled around on the ground for the rubber band she had dropped.

"I probably won't see you before the hunters, Kate," Tom laughed, making a quick escape as Rosie went to the rescue. "It's on the other side of the grounds to the jumping, so good luck."

"You too," she smiled.

Tom was eager to lose Georgina and quickly hurried away before she could tag along with him. Taking a deep breath, he looked at the jumps as they stretched out in front of him. It wasn't that they were enormous, it wasn't even that there were a lot of them, but it was a stiff course with so many difficult combinations – eleven jumps in all.

"Phew," Tom gasped, the adrenaline running through his body as he thought of what lay ahead.

Tom headed back to the van to find that his mother and father and Georgina's parents had arrived, and were gathered with the Sandy Lane group. Everyone was having lunch, even Georgina. Tom didn't know how she could eat anything. He felt sick with nerves.

"Hi Tom," said his Uncle Bob, holding out his hand. "Thanks for looking after Georgina's horse for us while we've been away. Apparently you've done a fantastic job with the brute."

Tom winced, hearing Chancey talked of in that way. Tom's mother looked at him sympathetically. She felt bad enough as it was that Georgina had taken Chancey away from him.

"You look so nice, Tom," she said, quickly changing the subject.

"Thanks Mom," he said looking down at his newly-pressed britches. He winced as he stretched his shoulders. Until that moment he had forgotten that his riding jacket, though good-looking, was far too small for him and extremely uncomfortable. He'd rather be wearing his old jeans any day.

"Georgina, have you walked the course yet?" he asked distractedly, staring into the distance.

"No, don't need to," said Georgina, her mouth crammed full of french fries, "I've seen it. Looks fine."

"Right," said Tom, shrugging his shoulders. "Well, I'm off to loosen up Feather. I'll be at the collecting ring if anyone wants me. The jumping's started."

"Good luck, Tom," Mrs. Buchanan called, as Tom walked over to Chancey.

"Good luck, boy," he whispered to Chancey, pulling his ears gently. Chancey nudged him playfully, shifting his weight lazily from one foot to the other as he basked in the sun.

Then Tom made his way to Feather and carefully tacked her up. One of her braids had come loose, so Tom quickly fixed it. Time was moving on and his butterflies were even worse now. He was sure that the horse would be able to feel the tension running through his body.

Quickly, he mounted and started to walk Feather toward the practice ring where lots of professional-looking riders were warming up their mounts. There were more than a hundred competitors in the open jumping class, the most popular event of the day. As Tom started to warm up Feather, Alex came riding past on Jester, a grin plastered on his face.

"Sixth," he called. Tom was pleased for him. Sixth was pretty good at a show of this standard and he felt encouraged by the result.

"There's hope for me yet then," Tom yelled back as Alex trotted on toward the pony club events.

And then there was an announcement over the loudspeaker that brought Tom back to earth with a jolt.

"Name change... number sixty-two, Horton Chancellor, owned by Robert Thompson, will be ridden by Georgina Thompson and number sixty-eight, Feather, owned by Sandy Lane Stables, will be ridden by Tom Buchanan," rang out over the loudspeaker.

Tom gritted his teeth and listened carefully to the numbers being announced. They were up to fifty-eight already. It would soon be Chancey's turn, and Georgina wasn't anywhere to be seen. Tom didn't usually like to watch anyone else riding the course. But he had to watch Chancey.

Jumping off Feather, he led her to the horse van and tied her to a ring before making his way to the stands. The crowd was quiet as competitor number sixty picked his way carefully around the course, finishing well within the three minute time limit. Tom stood away from his parents. He didn't want to hear any sympathetic noises when Georgina jumped Chancey. He was also in two minds about his feelings. He half-wanted Chancey to do well and yet he half-wanted Georgina to do badly.

Here they were now. Tom watched intently as Horton Chancellor was called into the ring and cantered a circle. Then they were off. Tom cringed as he heard the loud crack of the whip strike against Chancey's rump. Chancey looked equally displeased and almost leapt out of his skin with fright. He threw himself over the first jump, clearing it by miles. Georgina only just managed to regain her composure in time to sit still for the shark's teeth and the bank. They were over them, but at what a pace.

"Steady boy, steady," Tom breathed.

But it was too late, they were charging toward the combination, and now Georgina was kicking him on. Suddenly, she tried to check Chancey as he was about to jump the parallel. Tom closed his eyes as he heard the loud rap echo around the ring, but somehow the pole stayed up. They were rushing on to the triple. Georgina shortened her reins. Tom couldn't bear to look as Chancey struggled for his head and lurched over the three fences... clear.

She turned him stiffly toward the next jump. She wasn't going to be so lucky this time. There wasn't a moment for Chancey to gather impetus and, with a loud bang, he hit the gate which was sent crashing to the floor. Another loud whack resounded from Georgina's whip as Chancey headed for the last two jumps. Chancey lunged forward for the stile and staggered over it, his hooves just clipping the top. Then he reeled onto the gate. He was over it. But by the time he was through the finish, Chancey was foaming at the mouth and looked a nervous wreck. His body was lathered in sweat. Tom turned away in disgust at the sight of her parents congratulating her as the voice over the loudspeaker announced that competitor number sixty-two had four faults.

Tom tried to compose himself as he returned to Feather, eager to forget what he had seen. He figured out that they probably had about half an hour until it was their turn. Tom mounted and turned into the practice ring. He trotted Feather around and then, with a light nudge, took her into a gentle canter. She had a lovely loping stride, a very easy canter to ride. Gently, she glided over the post and rails that were set up as a practice jump.

"It won't be long now," he told her, patting her shoulder as he slowed her down. Calmly, Tom walked Feather around the ring to settle her as they awaited their turn. He could see another competitor come trotting out of the ring. All too suddenly it was upon them.

Once Tom was called into the ring, he told himself to block everything else out. They were here to do their best, and that was all they could do.

The bell rang out and they cantered to the first jump. Tom eased Feather over the brush, and they approached the shark's teeth. Deftly, she sprang over it. And now it was the bank. Taking it all in her stride, she rode onto it and down the other side. Tom swung her around wide to the combination, giving her enough room to look at it. He sat tight to the saddle, determined not to make the same mistakes Georgina had. Gently, he rode Feather to the middle of the jumps, steadying her as she sailed over them. He was so light with his hands, she could hardly have known he was there. Tom was starting to enjoy himself.

Leisurely, he faced her at the triple and they soared over the three jumps in succession. Again, he swooped around in a large circle to take Feather over the gate, the stile, the wall. Touch down! There was a loud cheer from the crowd as they left the ring. Tom clapped his hand to Feather's shoulder and buried his head in her mane.

"You were fantastic," he mumbled.

The voice on the loudspeaker announced the result.

"Tom Buchanan on Feather, jumping clear with no time faults."

"Way to go," Rosie called, jumping up and down with excitement.

Tom was going to have to wait until the jump-off, so he wandered over to where his parents were watching the rest of the competitors.

"Great job, Tom," his mother cried. She couldn't believe how well he had ridden.

"You took your time, Tom," Georgina sneered spitefully. "It must be easy to jump clear if you go at that snail's pace. You'll have to be a little faster next time if you don't want to be laughed out of the ring." Tom had to bite his tongue to stop himself from being very rude. Still Georgina went on.

"Horton Chancellor and I were kind of unlucky to hit that gate, weren't we?" she said, not waiting for a reply. "He overran it really. Still, less competition for you in the jump-off, eh?"

Tom was fuming, but he didn't have enough time to be angry, as the voice announced that there were ten riders through to the jump-off and the jumps were being raised that very moment. Tom rushed forward to watch.

The course was enormous now and speed was going to be crucial. He was the fifth one in. Not as good a position as he'd had at the local show, but still better than being first. The competition seemed pretty stiff. The other riders all looked as though they had been competing for years. Tom could hardly bear to watch, never mind listen, as the riders went into the ring and the results were announced. All of the times sounded very fast. Tom didn't have a clue what he needed to beat as he entered the ring for the second time. He would just have to go like the wind.

"Good luck," Rosie and Jess called from behind the fence.

Tom couldn't hear them though. The crowd hushed as he circled Feather.

And then they were off... racing to the first jump as the clock began ticking its countdown. They sailed over the brush, and then raced over the shark's teeth and soared over the bank. Feather's black eyes gleamed and her ears were pricked as she arched her neck. Her Arab lines were clearly defined as she stretched out her stride and raced forward. All Tom could see were the fences ahead of him, all he could hear was the sound of pounding hooves. Tom turned Feather to the combination. There were no wide swoops this time. The crowd gasped at the sharpness of the turn, but Feather knew what was expected of her and didn't even hesitate at the combination. Tom rode her at the middle of the jump, propelling her forward with his legs and she tucked her feet up under her as if the poles were hot pokers.

Again, Tom turned her immediately they touched the ground, so that there was hardly enough time for them to gather momentum. But he had judged it just right and Feather surged forward for the triple. One, two, three. Tom leaned forward in the saddle as the horse found her natural takeoff and swiftly cleared the fences. Now there were only three more jumps. It was all happening so quickly. Feather cantered on the spot, preparing herself for the last turn. Tom steadied her as they approached the gate. Cleared. Then they were on to the stile. Cleared. Now they were approaching the huge wall. They were over, and at what speed!

Tom could hardly contain himself as the voice from the loudspeaker announced that he had taken the lead with a time of one minute and four seconds. Tom clapped his hand to Feather's neck in excitement and neatly jumped to the floor.

"You were wonderful, Tom," called Jess, who had hardly been able to watch. "I bet you've won."

"No, someone's sure to beat me," he said. "There are still four competitors to go."

"I'm not so sure," said Nick, coming up behind them. "That will be a hard act to follow. Excellent job."

Tom walked Feather toward the trees to cool down for the result. He could hardly believe it, he had jumped clear. He didn't want to watch everyone else, it seemed unsportsmanlike to hope they wouldn't do well.

It seemed to take forever as the loudspeaker called out the times and repeatedly announced that Tom held the lead. There were only two more riders to go. Tom held his breath at the gasps from the crowd as the competitors thundered around the course. But no one matched his time.

Tom couldn't quite believe it when his name was called as the winner. Somehow, he found himself trotting forward.

The next thing Tom knew, he was flying around the ring again, this time with a blue ribbon pinned to Feather's bridle and a huge silver cup in his hands. Beams of light sprang off it as it glinted in the sunlight and they galloped their lap of honor. This had to be the greatest moment of his life.

As he came out of the ring, all of his friends from Sandy Lane gathered around him. He couldn't believe it... he, Tom Buchanan, was the winner of the open jumping at Benbridge. And then his heart sank as he remembered who he should have been riding.

"But it wasn't with Chancey," he said sadly to himself.

13

TO THE RESCUE

"I can't believe that Georgina's parents were actually pleased with her performance at Benbridge. She might as well have been wearing spurs. Chancey would have won the open jumping if Tom had been riding him." It didn't sound mean coming from Alex who never had a bad word to say about anyone.

"And she's a showoff if you ask me," said Jess, wrinkling up her nose.

"Worse than that. She will still be keeping Chancey at Sandy Lane too. It's really rubbing Tom's face in it." Alex brushed the last traces of sawdust from Hector's tail.

"Well, at least he gets to see Chancey," said Jess. "It would have been awful if she had taken him away. Tom's completely devoted to that horse. He's done so much with him. Do you remember what he was like when he first arrived at Sandy Lane?"

Jess and Alex were still chatting away when Tom passed behind them. Oblivious to the fact that he had heard every word, they continued with their tasks.

They were right of course, but even so, Tom was finding it difficult. He couldn't stop thinking about Chancey at Benbridge. The horse had been driven into a complete frenzy and Tom wasn't even in a position where he could say anything. He shouldn't have let himself get so attached to the horse. He hadn't meant to. It had just happened that way and he hadn't realized how hard it would be to give him up.

As Tom untacked Feather, he glanced around the stables. Everything was in order, everything was in its correct place. Except Chancey's door was wide open and swinging in the wind!

Bang! Ominously, it slammed shut.

No doubt that wretched Georgina had forgotten to bolt it. Tom hurried over and stuck his head around the door. The stall was empty – neither Chancey nor his tack were there.

Tom was puzzled. Georgina couldn't be riding in the woods – he had just been there on his ride. She hated practicing, so she wouldn't be in the outdoor arena. Still, it was worth a try. Tom ran down the drive to the outdoor arena. But there was no one there.

Then, as he turned back to the stables, it suddenly struck him. Georgina must have taken Chancey to the beach. Tom's heart sank as he remembered her impatience with the last coastal ride. She would love an opportunity to ride Chancey far out on the beach with no one to stop her. He looked at his watch and cringed. Four fifteen. He had a horrible feeling that it was high tide at five today. The beach would be almost covered by now.

Quickly, he ran to the tack room and looked at the tide sheet, breathlessly hoping that he was wrong. He felt the blood rushing to his head as he stared at the times before his eyes. Stupid girl.

"Nick, Nick," he cried, running to the house, desperately searching for help. But there was no one around. Where had Alex and Jess gone? There wasn't a moment to lose. Impulsively, he grabbed a bridle and ran to Feather's stall. He had no choice. He would have to go himself. Pulling the horse's head up out of her feed bucket, he put the bridle back on and led her out of the stall. There was no time for a saddle. He opened the gate and vaulted onto her back. Feather's neck was arched and her tail held high as she whinnied excitedly.

Tom turned her through the gate and pushed her on... faster and faster until they were galloping. Soon they were approaching the other side of the field. There wasn't time to stop and open the gate. He took a deep breath and prayed. Gritting his teeth as they went forward, he drove Feather toward the hedgerow. He grimaced as he heard the sharp twigs scratch her belly. He felt himself slipping and gripped harder with his knees. Feather took it as a command to go quicker and started to gallop over the stubble at a fast pace. Tom clung on for dear life as they raced through the woods, on and on to the open stretches beyond.

It was only when they were on the cliff tops that Tom drew Feather to a halt and looked down at the beach below. It was almost covered, except for a few remaining islands of sand left amid the surging, swirling sea. The silver, shimmering expanse of water stretched out in front of him.

Tom listened carefully. All he could feel was his heart beating faster, all he could hear was the ominous cry of the gulls overhead. He squinted into the distance. Perhaps they weren't here after all, he thought hopefully.

And then he heard a pitiful cry coming from a sand bar some way beyond Gull Rock. Straining his eyes, he could just make out a person and a horse, the water seeping in around them. The horse was sweating up and frantically swishing his tail. It had to be Georgina and Chancey.

"Georgina, Georgina!" Tom cried. Why didn't she guide Chancey toward the shore? It was probably still within their depth. In any case, horses were good swimmers. They could still make it if they were quick. Tom felt completely hopeless. What could he do? If he and Feather swam out to them, the tide would be higher still. They would never make it back. And he knew that he wasn't strong enough to swim it alone.

Then it came to him. If he rode around toward the headland, he could climb down the blowhole into the caves that he and Alex had explored last summer, and then wade across the rocks to the sand bar. Without hesitating, he gathered up Feather's reins and pushed her forward. Deftly she raced along the cliff tops to the far side of the bay, picking her way through the loose stones as she went. Tom dismounted. There was nowhere to tie her. He took a deep breath and knotted her reins. Then he slapped her rump and sent her on her way, hoping that she would find her way back to Sandy Lane and raise the alarm.

Soon he had found what he was looking for. Tom

shuddered as he looked down into the inky black abyss below him.

"Here goes," he said to himself. He knew that he could get down. He'd done it loads of times with Alex. But this was different – he had to be quick. One slip and he would go crashing to the bottom of the hole.

Tom looked down at his hands as he clutched at the stumps of grass. His knuckles were white, and his breath was coming faster now. Trembling, he climbed into the hole. He knew there were foot holds cut out of the rock. He would have to feel for them. Think of it as a ladder, he said to himself and carefully he struggled down and down.

When his foot finally touched water, he couldn't believe he had made it. Stepping down from the hole, he looked around him. He would have to pick his way out of the cave very cautiously. Holding onto weed and rocks to steady himself, he waded out against the waves until he was up to his hips.

"Georgina, Georgina," he called again. And this time she heard him. Her face was contorted with fear.

"Hang on. I'm coming for you," he said, calmly. One moment, the water was up to his waist, the next a wave rolled in and he was up to his neck. But he was nearly there. He would just have to swim the last part. It wasn't far. And then he reached the sand bar.

"Quickly, Georgina. There's not a moment to lose. The tide's still coming in. The sand bar will be covered before long."

"What do I do?" she wailed, the panic rising in her throat, her eyes white with fear. "Where did you come from?"

"Keep calm," said Tom. "I came from a cave over

there at the side of the cliff," he pointed. "If we can get back, then there's a hole you can climb up."

"No, no," she wailed. "I'm not going in the water. I'll drown. You should have gotten them to send a boat for me."

"Who? Get real, Georgina," said Tom. "There wasn't time for a boat. No one even knows you're here for one thing."

The sand bar had halved in size since he had first spotted them and they were quickly running out of time.

"Look, I'll swim to the cave and you hold onto my shoulders," Tom said, desperately trying to remember all he had learned in his lifesaving classes. Georgina seemed to calm down at this suggestion.

"OK, I'll hold onto you and you drag me," she said.

"Right," said Tom, getting more impatient by the minute. "Let's go."

"Chancey," he called. "Chancey, I'm coming back for you. Don't do anything silly." The horse was sidestepping around the sand bar, his eyes rolling uncontrollably.

Tom strode into the waves and plunged forward as Georgina held onto him. She was clinging on so tightly, that for a moment he panicked that she would drag him under. Once they had started, she calmed down though, and her grip slackened. Doggedly, Tom swam forward and forward until eventually they could stand.

"Stand Georgina, stand. Your feet can touch the bottom here. Walk forward." Quickly, he led her into the cave.

"Right, now this is the hole," he said pointing upward. "Up you go."

"I'm not going up there."

"Yes you are," Tom said firmly. "Or you'll drown."

"I need you to show me how to do it," Georgina cried hysterically.

"I've got to go back for Chancey, Georgina."

"Never mind the horse," she screamed. "What about *me*?" Tom looked at her in disbelief.

"I'll drown," she said. "He's only a horse, he can be replaced."

Tom looked out to sea at the familiar figure still struggling on the sand bar, now a silhouette against the bleak horizon.

"No," he said firmly. "I'm going back. If I guide him, we can swim to the path. I got you this far. Once you're on the top of the cliffs, you'll be safe. You know the way back."

"It's dangerous," Georgina yelled.

But Tom didn't listen as he turned and headed back into the sea. It wasn't long before he was up to his neck. He spluttered as he took in a gulp of water. Moving his arms was nearly impossible as the weight of his sweatshirt dragged him down. Out of breath, he scrambled onto the sand bar and quickly grabbed Chancey's bridle.

"Come on boy. We're going to get off here. We're going to be all right. You've got to swim to the shore – straight ahead, toward the path. I know that it looks a long way, but you're strong. You can do it."

Tom had a job keeping Chancey still as he scrambled on top of him. Chancey circled the sand bar and pawed at the ground.

Tom patted his shoulder to settle him down. Then he urged him forward and they plunged into the waves.

When Chancey realized that he could swim, he wasn't so frightened. But in spite of his words of encouragement, Tom really didn't know if they could make it. Chancey was a courageous horse, but two hundred yards was a long way to swim.

They seemed to make good progress at first, but after the first five minutes, Chancey was beginning to struggle. The current was stronger than Tom had anticipated and he felt exhausted as he clung on, gripping until his legs were numb. Were they nearly halfway now? Tom didn't know. Surely they must be. But the shore didn't seem to be any closer. Bravely, they battled forward. Chancey snorted and spluttered as the water swirled, until slowly, the shore grew larger. They were getting closer. Tom started to feel more positive. Surely they could make it now. He thought he heard voices carried to him on the sea air. They were almost there.

And suddenly they must have hit the sand. Chancey's nostrils were a fiery red as he forced his way through the crashing waves. He seemed to be walking along the seabed. They were at the foot of the cliffs. Tom felt shivery as they reached the path. He slid to the ground, unable to hold on any longer and everything went black...

14

CHANCEY FOREVER!

Nick was startled when Feather clattered into the stables, her reins dangling broken by her sides, her coat dank with sea water. His heart sank. She had come from the beach. Someone was in danger. He looked at his watch. He looked at the tide sheet. Someone was in serious danger.

There wasn't a moment to lose. Nick hurried over to where Whispering Silver was basking lazily in the sun and climbed into the saddle. Turning out of the stables, he called to Sarah to bring the truck around the old coastal track to the top of the cliffs. There wasn't time to answer any questions.

Slipping through the back gate, he headed for the cliffs, taking the same route Tom had taken no more than half an hour ago... through the fields, through the woods, to the open stretches beyond.

Nick reached the path at the top of the cliffs at a

quarter to five just as Georgina was scrambling her way up the blowhole.

Nick gazed anxiously out to sea, willing himself to see something... anything. But there wasn't anyone around. Or was there? And then he saw it – the outline of a horse on a sand bar. He looked harder. It looked like Chancey, but where was his rider? Now he could see a tiny speck moving halfway between the cliffs and the sand bar. Nick craned his neck farther forward. It seemed to be getting closer to the sand. It was a person. And then he saw someone else on the far side of the cliffs. It looked like Georgina.

"What on earth is going on?" he bellowed. "Who's that on the sand bar?"

"Ch...Ch...Chancey," Georgina stuttered.

"I can see that," he said. "But who's that out there with him?"

"Tom."

"*Tom.*" Nick was flabbergasted. "What's he doing out there?"

"It's... it's my fault," Georgina spluttered, shivering now from both cold and fear. "I got caught and he wanted to go back for the horse. They will be able to make it won't they? They will be all right?"

"Well, we'll soon see," Nick said grimly, scrambling down the path to the beach where the waves were crashing fiercely against the rocks.

It was a long way to swim. Nick had never felt so completely powerless. All he could do was watch. The pair seemed to be progressing slowly. And then he heard the noise of a car engine and Sarah appeared at the top of the cliffs. As she hurried down the path to join Nick, she needed no explanation. Training her eyes on the moving figures, she held her breath. The current was so strong but they were about halfway now. Could they make the shore?

"Clever boy," Sarah was saying. "He's following an angled route to take account of the currents."

Nick's mind was whirling. He couldn't watch. He couldn't stop watching. He couldn't think straight. He didn't know what to do. Turning from the sea, he listened to Sarah's running commentary. And he couldn't stop himself from looking back and remembering the day he had first met Tom. Had it come to this?

"They've only got fifty yards or so to go," said Sarah.

Nick snapped out of his trance as he realized that he hadn't been listening to a word Sarah had been saying. He rushed forward as Chancey clawed at the rocks and stumbled up the path. Tom collapsed at his feet.

* * * * * * * * * * * * * * *

When Tom awoke, he was back in his bedroom at home. The curtains were drawn, but as his eyes became accustomed to the dark, he could just make out the shape of the large china horse on his bookshelf. Perhaps it had all been a dream. He reached up to his forehead. There was something on it, something cold and damp. It felt like a washcloth.

Tom's head felt fuzzy. His heart started to beat faster

as slowly it all started to come back to him.

"Mom, Mom, where are you?" He was panicking now. Mrs. Buchanan rushed into the room.

"Why am I in bed?" he cried. "Where's Chancey? Did it all really happen?"

"Calm down Tom," his mother said sensibly. "One question at a time. Everything's OK. You're just exhausted. Yes, it did all happen and you hit your head when you fell."

"But Georgina," said Tom.

"She's fine," said his mother. "In disgrace, but fine. She managed to climb up the blowhole. And Chancey's all right too. Showing off, but still in one piece. You've slept through the night, so you haven't missed out on anything."

"Oh," said Tom, a wave of relief spreading right through him. "I shouldn't have saved Georgina, should I?" he joked. "Then I would have had Chancey all to myself."

"You were extremely brave," said his mother. "A lot has happened since then. You might find you have a few surprises," she said, drawing back the curtains. "Look outside."

Tom's head ached as he leaned out of his bed and looked out of the window. Then he laughed, for there was Chancey, walking on Mrs. Buchanan's flower garden. Alex was holding onto his halter and waving up at Tom.

"What's going on Mom?" he said, stifling a giggle as Chancey pawed at Mrs. Buchanan's prizewinning dahlias. Mrs. Buchanan frowned.

"Well, I think your visitor will explain," she said mysteriously, as the door opened and Georgina entered looking shamefaced.

"I'll leave you two alone," said Mrs. Buchanan. She smiled encouragingly at Georgina as she let herself out of the room. Nervously, Georgina approached the side of Tom's bed.

"What are you here for?" he asked, bemused.

"Just hear me out, Tom," said Georgina. "I know what I did was foolish," she stammered. "I thought I knew best."

Tom couldn't believe what he was hearing. His cousin Georgina was standing in front of him, admitting she had been in the wrong. Was he dreaming? He sat up and rubbed his eyes.

"I can't thank you enough," Georgina went on. "You saved my life... I'm sorry for being so awful. And I want you to have him."

Tom looked up and caught her gaze.

"Who?" said Tom.

"Chancey," she said.

"Chancey?" Tom spluttered. It was the last thing he had expected. "You mean you're giving him to me? Are you crazy?"

"Maybe a little," Georgina smiled. "But I don't want to ride any more. I only took it up because I thought Daddy wanted me to. Now it turns out he would have been as happy for me to do ballet," she laughed. "So, if you want him." She hesitated, waiting for Tom to answer her. "We would like him to go to a good home."

"Want him... *Want him*?" said Tom, getting more excited by the minute. "I can't believe what I'm hearing. Things like this don't really happen. Tell me I'm not dreaming."

And, as if in response, there was a loud whinny

from the backyard. It was as though Chancey was trying to tell Tom what he thought about it all. He was Tom's horse forever now, he seemed to be saying... not just for the summer.

The Runaway Pony by Susannah Leigh

The second title in the Sandy Lane Stables series

Angry shouting and the crunch of hooves on gravel made Jess spin around sharply. Careering towards her, wild-eyed with fear and long tail flying behind, was a palomino pony. It was completely out of control. Jess's heart began to pound and her breath came in sharp gasps, but almost without thinking she held out her arms...

When the riderless palomino pony clatters into the yard, no one is more surprised than Jess. Hot on the pony's hooves comes a man waving a head collar. Jess helps him catch the pony and sends them on their way. Little is she to know what far-reaching consequences her simple actions will have...

Strangers at the Stables by Michelle Bates

The third title in the Sandy Lane Stables series

... Thoughts jostled around in Rosie's mind as she crossed the yard. She couldn't believe how many things had gone wrong. She needed time to think. There was something worrying her, right at the back of her mind. Something that held the key to it all. But what was it?

When the owners of Sandy Lane have to go away, everyone still expects the stables to run smoothly in their absence. No one is quite prepared for all the things that happen over the next few weeks. There isn't time to get help, the children of Sandy Lane have to act fast, if they want to save their stables...